T0151146

MAGICAL TALES

THE NEW ADVENTURES OF HELEN

Magical Tales

Ludmilla Petrushevskaya

translated by Jane Bugaeva

DEEP VELLUM PUBLISHING
DALLAS, TEXAS

Deep Vellum Publishing
3000 Commerce St., Dallas, Texas 75226
deepvellum.org · @deepvellum

Deep Vellum is a 501c3 nonprofit literary arts organization
founded in 2013 with the mission to bring
the world into conversation through literature.

Support for this publication has been provided in part by the Mikhail
Prokhorov Fund's Transcript Program, the National Endowment for
the Arts, and Amazon Literary Partnership.

ISBNs: 978-1-64605-103-8 (paperback) | 978-1-64605-104-5 (ebook)

LIBRARY OF CONGRESS CONTROL NUMBER: 2021944452

Exterior design by Natalya Balnova | natalyabalnova.com

Interior Layout and Typesetting by KGT

Printed in the United States of America

CONTENTS

THE NEW ADVENTURES OF HELEN

AS WE ALL KNOW, HELEN OF TROY is reborn once every thousand years. On the night of one such reappearance, when she was to emerge from the sea-foam onto the shore of a particular seaside resort, a little mirror appeared in one of the resort's market stalls. The mirror was magic—whoever looked in it would become invisible.

The mirror was crafted by the resort town's local wizard—a drunkard and a show-off who spent many nights pondering the fate of the world, reading old newspapers and books, soldering, sharpening, gluing, and stargazing. This wizard had calculated the exact time of Helen's rebirth. The wizard didn't like women (or men, for that matter); he respected only sick children and the elderly, despite their whining and bad tempers, and was thinking of them when he fabricated the magic mirror for Helen. In times of war, the first people to die are always children and the elderly, and Helen's rebirth was always followed by long, brutal wars, not to mention unpleasantries like the annihilation of entire nations.

The wizard spent an entire year carving the mirror out of crystal before covering one side in liquid silver. He was careful never to look into the mirror himself; instead, he went to the town square and held the mirror up to a statue to catch its reflection. The statue immediately vanished.

It disappeared without going anywhere.

Everyone just stopped noticing it—it was forgotten.

The next morning, once he'd sobered up, the wizard tinkered with the mirror a bit more (gluing here, filing there) and dripped a single drop from a black potion bottle onto its surface. This drop imbued the mirror with one final power: if the mirror were ever broken, the entities whose reflections it held would become visible again.

Deep down, the wizard was a good person, but humanity irritated him so much that he'd sometimes run out on the street to yell, stomp, and wave his arms about. The last time he'd done this was after a poor young simpleton's house had burned down. The neighbors had to pull the simpleton out of the flames because she was hellbent against parting with her couch. And while some neighbors fought the fire, others surreptitiously harvested apples and plums from her orchard (they would've baked anyway) and lugged basketfuls to their pantries, barns, cellars, and sheds. The wizard himself had done nothing to help the simpleton—he wasn't the Red Cross, ready to lend a hand at a moment's notice. He didn't concern himself with the little things; let people mend their own fences, he thought. And anyway, the simpleton was no innocent weakling; she regularly beat up her elderly aunt who lived across the street, and no one ever intervened.

The simpleton spent the rest of the day sitting on the front lawn of her charred house, and only in the evening did one kind woman take pity on the girl and invite her over for dinner. In need of somewhere to spend the night, the simpleton knocked on her aunt's door. Her aunt, despite being eighty-five, hadn't forgotten the frequent beatings and was generally terrified of her niece. Normally she wouldn't answer the door, but this time she opened up saying, "Take a hike," and then added, "to the bath-house," which was roomy and had a wood-burning stove. Mind you, the aunt was no saint either and used to steal chickens in her youth, and the seemingly kind woman who fed the simpleton dinner was quite abusive to her older sister, spreading awful rumors about her: "She never washes the dishes—is she royalty or just a slob?"

Now, those indiscretions are lesser known, but every-one heard about the pilfering on the day of the fire thanks to the wizard, who spent that evening at the pub ranting about crime and punishment and promising that those apples and plums would end up choking someone. His two longtime girlfriends nodded in agreement—the elderly, heavily made-up women had plenty of qualms with the townspeople themselves (and the townspeople, especially the female contingent, with them). All his raving at the pub resulted in a line of people outside the aunt's house the next morning, offering old sweaters, silk dresses, and winter coats (with the fur collars removed, of course)— generous gifts for the fire victim from her kind neighbors. So that's a bit about the local mores of this particular seaside town.

But back to Helen.

The wizard had found an antidote to Helen's beauty, but how would this gorgeous—but utterly stupid—newborn woman stumble upon the mirror? That was a detail the wizard needed to iron out. What if Helen were to buy the mirror at the market? For a woman to not be drawn to a market was inconceivable. This, the wizard had gotten absolutely right.

And so the night of Helen's rebirth had arrived. The beginning was quite ordinary: Helen walked out of the sea in her birthday suit—she could've been just another nighttime swimmer, bathing nude under the starlight. The wizard didn't go out to greet her. He was afraid her incredible beauty would make him lose his mind and magic. He wasn't about to abandon his life to go chasing blindly after

Helen—the exact fate that awaited any man who saw her. You see, ranks of men would follow Helen: a pack would form, the back rows would start to worm their way forward, the men in front would elbow those in back, who'd respond in kind without hesitation, and so on, until, inevitably, war would break out.

All that to say, Helen was reborn unnoticed. She came upon a pile of clothes some swimmer had left, slowly dried herself with their towel, put on their robe and slippers, picked up their purse, and headed toward town without a second thought about the fate of the woman who would emerge from the sea five minutes later finding nothing but a wet towel crumpled on the sand. That's just how it goes with beautiful women—they don't think about consequences. Plus, what can you expect from someone who is but five minutes old?

Apart from beauty, the only thing the foam-born goddess had in spades was a curiosity and an eagerness to learn from other women, picking out what she deemed to be their best qualities. But there were few other women on the dark side street that led away from the sea: just an elderly Cat Lady who sat on a stool surrounded by her flock and a middle-aged woman standing under the street's lone streetlight.

The Cat Lady glared at Helen and mumbled, "Here comes trouble," while the cats, each considering itself to be the Helen of the pack, calmly groomed themselves—truth be told, the cats would've been good role models for Helen, but she didn't notice them. Instead she walked toward the streetlight, where the middle-aged woman had just extracted a pocket-mirror and a black eyeliner pencil from her purse. For the first time in her life, Helen stood before a Woman (the Cat Lady didn't count). Helen watched the Woman meticulously draw on black eyebrows—two huge, sideways commas facing each other—they made the Woman look ferocious. Helen froze in awe. But the Woman wasn't finished. Next, she outlined her eyes—these, she drew in the shape of fish. She returned the eyeliner to her purse, got out a tube of lipstick, and coated her lips with thick strokes of red. She smacked her lips to evenly distribute the color and then added red arcs above and below her natural lips, making them appear five times bigger. The Woman looked in her mirror and said with satisfaction, "Full facial reconstruction!" Lastly, she reddened the apples of her cheeks, checking the mirror once more before she dropped her tools back into her purse.

Needless to say, Helen's ruby mouth was agape as she marveled at the Woman. To Helen, she was the epitome of beauty: heavy black brows, dark eyes, huge red lips, and a single gold tooth. And when Helen saw the Woman light a cigarette and insert it to the left of her gold tooth, it was a done deal—the foam-born goddess understood exactly how she needed to look.

Helen approached the Woman.

"Beat it, before you get your bell rung," said the articulate stranger.

"Hello?" said Helen, not understanding.

"Hello, anybody home?" mocked the Woman.

Confused, Helen fell silent.

"Who ditched you here, jailbait? I'm older than your mother!" said the Woman bitterly.

Helen stared at the Woman in wonder.

"Whatcha starin' at? Get outta my spotlight." The Woman sneered, added a few more incomprehensible phrases, and finished with, "this is my corner." Helen walked off, baffled, but made sure to avoid the other street-lights—there was someone in the "spotlight" under each one, as the Woman had put it.

As she walked on, Helen felt around the contents of her purse and found an eyeliner, some lipstick, and a wallet with a bit of money. But the night swimmer hadn't packed a mirror. Though Helen was as dumb as a door-nail, she understood that something was missing—something to look into. She fiddled with the lipstick and eyeliner, and the desire to be as beautiful as the Woman under the streetlight made her head spin. And she desperately wanted a gold tooth.

§

Thanks to her spa attire, no one paid much attention to Helen, with the exception of a billionaire who'd come to vacation at the seaside resort all by himself (i.e., with only his security detail, no girlfriends); yes, he'd noticed the young girl in a bathrobe and slippers sitting under a tree at sunrise, rummaging through her purse, counting the two bills in the palm of her hand. At one point she lifted her head, glancing upward in concentration, and suddenly everything was bathed in a blinding golden light. But this miracle was short-lived because the girl quickly lowered her head once more, apparently having calculated the sum of one plus one. The billionaire, an athletic young man, rushed downstairs without his bodyguards but was stopped by his driver, who'd been radioed by the security detail, so by the time he was escorted outside by his retinue, the girl had disappeared. All that remained was a sparkle in the air and the lingering scent of a thunderstorm.

As for Helen, she walked down the street looking for something reflective. There weren't any puddles, only gasoline spills. And even she sensed that it would be rude to apply makeup in the window of a storefront or apartment. But Helen was a woman through and through, and she soon made an observation: all the women of the town were heading in the same direction. The current swelled as small streams of women flowed in from side streets, and Helen hurried along with them until she finally found herself in front of a huge market square.

Helen watched how the women behaved: they walked around, stopped at certain stalls, and asked, "how much?" then dug in their wallets, sweated, stressed, counted, and handed over money, received bundles, parcels, boxes, and bags, then tried on shoes, and so on. Helen felt alive! She clutched her wallet as she moved through the crowded street and finally spotted a small mirror in one of the stalls.

"Hello. How much?" she said in a still-unfamiliar voice. The merchant casually looked up at Helen but, upon seeing her, he immediately turned red, his eyes grew wide, and he sputtered, "Take whatever you want for free, my dear! Take me!" Just then, the merchant's wife turned around and saw Helen and her husband's crimson nape, and so began one of those petty but lengthy marital squabbles of which the wizard was so weary. Helen ran off but the harm had been done: the merchant raced after her, and his wife and mother-in-law raced after him, followed by every other male merchant—they'd all abandoned their stalls and joined the procession. But Helen would not have been a bona fide woman had she not been clutching the mirror in her hand—she'd heard the merchant's first offer ("Take whatever you want for free!") and snatched up the treasure. Now she ran ahead of the enormous mob until they were all stopped short by a police officer.

"What's going on?" he barked, grabbing his baton.

"Thief!" panted the merchant's wife. "She stole a mirror!"

"It was a gift! She's no thief!" cried the merchant desperately. "A gift for the woman who stole my heart!"

But his wife had already grabbed Helen's beautiful hair in one hand and the mirror in the other. All the men rushed to defend the innocent beauty, but Helen squealed and took matters into her own hands—she bit the hand clutching the mirror and smacked the merchant's wife on the head with her purse, setting herself free. The officer, finally getting a good look at Helen, turned the color of beet soup and began shrilly blowing his whistle while reflexively smacking people with his baton. The mob shifted, forming a circle around Helen, and everyone stared at her, transfixed. And that's when Helen—surrounded by a golden glow, rosy-cheeked and curly haired, eyes flashing in pain—lifted the mirror to her face to see what damage the merchant's wife had done. And instantly, the golden light went out and everyone lost interest in her.

The magic mirror had worked! Helen looked up and saw all the men walking away. War had been averted.

Helen left the market undisturbed and sat down in a small park where, armed with the black eyeliner and red lipstick, she began—as her first earthly acquaintance had called it—her "full facial reconstruction." Helen drew two commas over her eyebrows, fishtails on her eyes, and a red heart around her lips, and then she rouged the apples of her cheeks. She searched on the ground and found a discarded gold chocolate wrapper, tore off a small piece, and wrapped the foil around her front tooth. She stared in the mirror, unable to take her eyes off her own magnificent reflection—she bared her gold tooth, pursed her lips, and whispered, "Beat it, jailbait, this is my corner." She found a cigarette butt on the ground and put it between her red lips, all the while looking in the mirror. Finally satisfied, she got up and strolled through town with the same seductive swagger the Woman had used to circle her streetlight.

But no one noticed Helen!

If it weren't for the mirror, Helen, made-up in this way, would've caused quite the war—complete with sieges, bombing raids, and espionage. The Commander in Chief would've kept her as his private radio operator in a far-off bunker, and Helen would've looked stunning in her khaki skirt, soldier's blouse, side cap, and ankle boots. And with those black brows and rosy cheeks! But the mirror left this particular region at peace as Helen continued to go unnoticed. In fact, she wasn't even noticed when she walked into a corner store and grabbed some bread and a bottle of water. She walked out chewing the bread and then, her appetite awoken (Helen hadn't eaten since birth), walked into a restaurant and sat down. The waiter, oblivious to her presence, set the table and brought over some food simply by force of habit. Helen enjoyed a wonderful lunch, then got up and left.

Helen was a bit disappointed by her debut. Of course, she didn't like being the cause of endless brawls, altercations, and riots. She hated it when men gawked at her and fought with their wives over their right to give her gifts. And she couldn't stand it when said wives clawed at her hair and face. Usually, such impossible beauties had only two ways out: to drink themselves ugly as fast as possible or become actors—which, in the end, yielded the same result. Yes, being beautiful wasn't easy. But being completely unnoticed was no picnic, either.

So Helen paused to think for the first time in her life and tried to figure out why she was failing to attract the attention she deserved. Her first thought was that all men were idiots. Who wouldn't notice these brows, these cheeks, a gold tooth? But then, being quite observant, Helen began actually observing women. When a couple walked down the street, Helen would look at the woman, not the man. In clothing stores, she followed beautiful women around, went into dressing rooms with them, and watched as they tried on clothes from a corner. At restaurants, she didn't just ogle women, she walked right up to them and even felt the fabric of their dresses (they didn't notice a thing). After an hour, she came to a remarkable conclusion: not all women were made-up like the Woman under the streetlight. Almost all of them walked and smoked like her, but their clothes and makeup were different. Their décolletages didn't plunge to their belly buttons, and their dresses weren't so short that they couldn't lift their arms without causing scandal (when a woman lifts her arms, her dress rides up; Helen deduced that some women did this on purpose to draw attention to themselves). And perhaps the Woman's heels were too high—when she walked, one leg had worked fine while the other kept giving out. What's more, Helen never saw another gold tooth, so she removed her foil.

Helen's self-education was in full swing. She visited five clothing stores and dressed herself from head to toe without being noticed; at a salon, she wiped off her makeup and applied some high-end face creams without asking. She threw out the eyeliner and lipstick but kept the mirror tucked away in her purse. From time to time, she looked in it and saw her exquisite, cleanly washed face, but still no one noticed her.

Couples strolled and dined together, while single men and women walked past one another, seemingly uninterested (even though it was a resort with perfume in the air, sea mist, feathered hats, taut silks, alluring horizons, and so on). Such are the unspoken rules of resorts: those who are searching for love rarely find it, while those who aren't, do. Helen, however, was oblivious to such things.

By evening, she had grown tired and returned to the same tree where she'd sat that morning, counting someone else's money in her bathrobe and slippers. Now she wore a blue silk dress and a white brimmed hat and her legs were aching.

At that same moment, the lonely billionaire stepped out on the balcony of his mansion across the street and stared longingly at Helen—rather, at the empty spot under the tree where Helen's divine presence had been that morning. Helen thought that he'd noticed her and suddenly became quite flustered—she blushed, she was bathed in golden light from head to toe, and her unbearably bright eyes flashed in the direction of the balcony.

If the billionaire had been one of millions offering Helen his heart on a platter, she wouldn't have paid him any attention. But in that moment, he was the sole person who'd noticed her, and in the land of the blind the one-eyed man is king. So Helen made an effort: she focused her gaze on the first star above the mountains, a bit to the left of the billionaire, then she looked down at her sandals, and finally, just for a second, looked at her object of interest—and in response the billionaire yawned, rubbed his eyes, and went back inside. Helen was utterly confused.

Idiot, she thought miserably. Her golden light went out. Why don't I go live in his mansion? I've got to live somewhere. Of course, this was just an excuse: Helen had fallen in love with the only man who had looked right at her and yawned (everyone else turned scarlet).

No sooner said than done: the invisible Helen slipped past every obstacle on the way to her beloved as easily as a hot knife cuts through butter. She walked past the security detail goofing off with their guns and watching TV, past the secretary sitting behind twenty phones and watching TV, and followed a lackey, who was bringing the dogs in after dinner, through a security-coded door into the billionaire's bedroom. He was lying in a bed the size of a tennis court, also watching TV. Helen lay down next to him and, naturally, began watching TV. It was her first time watching a Mexican soap opera—she cried at the end of the episode, she liked it so much.

The billionaire was scheduled to eat dinner at a casino, per the contract he'd signed with the resort over a year ago (billionaire's lives are always planned years in advance). At the casino, he was to lose a hundred grand, receive a digital watch as a consolation prize, then gift the watch to a cabaret soloist. Next, the billionaire was to dance with the soloist, invite her to dinner (which was to be filmed by the TV station CMN International), and end the night together at a club. Everything was paid for—the billionaire's very presence was a publicity stunt. He couldn't just go somewhere at his leisure, just give a woman flowers, just swim in the sea—everything would be immediately filmed and end up on TV or in the papers.

The billionaire got dressed, Helen followed him into his limo, and soon they arrived at the casino. But then everything went awry: Helen was rooting for the billionaire and stopped the roulette wheel exactly where he'd placed his bet. No one noticed the charade because Helen turned out to be quite clever and slowed the wheel gradually. And so, after collecting his hundred thousand in winnings, the billionaire did not receive a consolation prize and had nothing to give the expectant cabaret soloist and no reason to invite her to dance. But the music began to play as scheduled, and Helen stepped into the billionaire's arms, and he started twirling around the dance floor completely alone. The way he gently pulled his imaginary partner close was so realistic that the delighted CMN producer ran the footage on every channel, and everyone said it was the perfect pantomime—the billionaire even kissed his imaginary partner's hand! The whole ordeal was incredibly profitable. No one knew that the billionaire was so talented. He had long been considered a total idiot who'd lucked out and found a quick way to get rich.

Everyone applauded wildly and the billionaire bowed awkwardly, thinking he'd completely lost his mind: he'd just been clutching the most tender, wonderful, intangible woman, who smelled of the best perfume in the world (it goes without saying that when Helen took the perfume from the store, simply liking its scent, she had no idea that a single bottle cost as much as an oceanfront house). The billionaire smiled and looked around—was someone playing a joke on him?

Next, the billionaire was supposed to take the soloist to a nightclub, but as the middle-aged cabaret star approached him, someone stepped on the train of her dress. It ripped right off—the star turned at the sound of splitting fabric, saw only her undies, and disappeared behind the nearest window drape like a moon slips behind a cloud—there one minute, gone the next. Thus the billionaire headed to his limo all by himself. But when he shut the door, he felt light-headed; Helen was sitting next to him and he smelled her perfume again.

"Let's go home," she said, giggling quietly.

The billionaire didn't hear her voice or laughter, and he didn't discover anyone next to him no matter how much he groped at the air around him, but suddenly his limo turned around and, instead of going to the nightclub, drove him home to his TV and his three dogs, who were already asleep on his tennis court–sized bed.

That night the billionaire had a wonderful dream: Helen sat under the tree on the shore while he knelt beside her, they braided flowers into wreaths and played checkers, she wore a robe and slippers, her tangled curls fell across her pink face, and a golden light streamed down her slender arms.

The billionaire fell into a strange depression. He began neglecting his duties, stopped showing up to press conferences, quit horseback riding and playing golf—he was only ever seen at the casino, where he would win 100K every night and then head home. Helen would eat from his plate and sleep in his bed—she slept five yards away from him on the far end beside the dogs, who, by the way, had grown to love her. When the lackeys would let them out, she'd run outside, too, and the dogs would jump with glee. Afterward, the billionaire would greet them all as if after a long separation.

But this couldn't go on forever.

Helen liked the lifestyle—she was warm, well fed, entertained (the Mexican soap opera was on every night), her love was by her side, and there was no grabbing, no blushing like a beet, no lustful panting, no kidnapping, no brawling. She was causing no battles and no wars.

But the billionaire was losing his mind. He had reoccurring dreams about the simple girl wearing a robe and slippers and holding two bills in her hand. He fantasized about finding her and showering her with gold, buying her a gown adorned with pearls, taking her everywhere and showing her off. And later, she'd bear his children and they'd live on an island and so on. He wept. He pined.

All the while, the wizard sat in his cave, rubbing his hands together: any day now, the billionaire would sign away his fortune to the needy and jump off his balcony to the foot of the tree he stared at every evening.

But there isn't a woman in the world, who, having fallen in love, can't find a way to the object of her affection.

So one night, Helen went to see the only woman she knew—that's to say she went to the coastal alley where she'd first met the Woman. The Woman was shuffling under her streetlight in the whistling autumn wind. She wore a ragged fur jacket and the Cat Lady watched her bitterly from across the street—she suspected that jacket bore the unfortunate fates of a dozen cats. Helen stood under the streetlight.

"Who's there?" The Woman asked, then answered herself, "This isn't a knock-knock joke." She yawned, adding, "Can't throw a brick without hitting a workin' girl."

"Hello!" said Helen.

"Life's a tough row to hoe," said the Woman,

shivering. Another woman came out of the shadows, stout as a mountain, wearing a similar ratty fur jacket with a short red skirt and thigh-high crimson boots.

"Who're you talking to?" she asked.

The Cat Lady swayed angrily on her stool and scooped some cats up onto her lap.

"To myself," said the Woman. "I should go to the wizard, ask him for a cure for old age. Or for his magic mirror. Live my life in peace without being noticed. He was hollerin' about makin' such a mirror. Braggin' that he'd stopped a war. But he doesn't have it anymore, some broad named Helen's got it. But she's invisible, so he can't find it. Whoever looks in the mirror becomes invisible!"

"Why would you want that?" asked the portly woman. "That's like dying!"

"When he was all boozed up, the wizard told Anya that breaking the mirror brings the person back. 'Cause she'd asked, 'Who'd want to be invisible forever?' and he'd said, 'No, not forever.'"

At that exact moment, they heard breaking glass and someone wrapped up in a luxurious men's bathrobe appeared in the shadow of a tree. The women screeched.

"Who's there? Enough with the monkey business!" the Woman said, then sighed with relief after seeing Helen.

"There's the mirror you want," said Helen.

The fat woman picked the largest shard up off the ground, instinctively brought it to her face, and disappeared. The Woman lunged at the broken mirror pieces glimmering in the glow of the streetlight, crying, "Me too, me too!"

She looked into a tiny sliver of glass and evaporated.

Helen paused in thought, then picked up the last mirror fragment and put it in her pocket.

The next morning the billionaire went out on his balcony, as he always did, and looked down at the tree. He saw a bustling crowd. Three men were brawling, the rest were yelling, and in the middle of it all stood that same young girl with the pink face and golden curls, looking up at him. A police officer was holding her by the hand. The billionaire cursed and ran from his balcony. It took him five minutes to get past his own security and by then the crowd was already dispersing. Paramedics were tending to two injured men and some grannies stood off to the side recapping the fight.

"Where's the girl?" asked the billionaire. The grannies looked at him suspiciously and walked away. A search of the jails and police stations yielded nothing. Witnesses said there had been a girl but whether she ran off or what, no one knew.

So the billionaire got hold of a rope ladder and tied it to the railing of his balcony unbeknownst to his security detail. He waited for the girl to reappear. But autumn smoothly gave way to a wet, muddy winter, and still no one appeared under the tree. Even the TV reporters left the resort.

"Maybe I should just hang myself?" the billionaire once wondered out loud. "I can't leave this town, she's here somewhere—I can feel it! Can you hear me? I would die if it meant seeing you!"

Suddenly a sunbeam danced on his face, as if someone was reflecting the sun into his eyes. He understood that an invisible presence was sending him a signal from under the tree. He lowered his rope ladder and climbed down from his balcony, for once unaccompanied. A small mirror fragment floated in the air. The billionaire grabbed it and instinctively looked at his reflection. He screamed, unheard by anyone. Next to him stood the girl, smiling.

No one saw the billionaire ever again. He had disappeared without leaving a will and since he was never found, dead or alive, his fortune remained in the bank under his name. An investigation found that the TV crew had bribed his entire security detail to never let the billionaire out of the house without alerting them first. The investigation also found a rope ladder hanging from the billionaire's balcony and six house-slipper footprints. Nothing else of interest was found.

But some police informers reported that the wizard spent the night drinking alone at the pub and wouldn't let anyone join his table, even though there were two empty chairs. And in his drunken state he spoke to the empty chairs, clinked glasses with their invisible inhabitants, and complimented their outfits and hats.

As for the magic mirror: maybe Helen keeps it in her pocket so that, one day, she and the billionaire can return to this world—though nobody has heard anything about them as of yet.

Maybe they live in an imperial palace on some island, invisible to all, flying on planes and sailing on yachts. Maybe they're happy and fulfilled because no one is exploiting them for money or stalking them with cameras or kidnapping them or starting wars in their names. And once they've quietly grown old, maybe they'll smash the mirror and reappear in the world—just an unremarkable elderly couple—and settle down in a small town.

Maybe. But not anytime soon.

NOSE GIRL

THERE ONCE LIVED A VERY BEAUTIFUL GIRL named Nina. She had curly golden hair, big sea-blue eyes, and brilliant white teeth. When she laughed, it felt like the sun was shining; when she cried, her tears looked like pearls falling down her face. There was only one thing that tarnished her good looks—her huge nose.

One day, Nina gathered up all the money she had and went to a doctor.

"I have no one in this town," she told him. "I earn my own living and my mother and father live far away, so I can't ask them for money—they aren't rich anyway. This is all the money I've got. Please make my nose smaller! My parents made a mistake when I was born: they threw a party to celebrate but forgot to invite an old sorcerer who lived in the woods. When he found out he hadn't been invited, he was very upset and promised to give me an important and valuable present. From that day, my nose began to grow. My parents pleaded with the sorcerer, but he insisted that if I grew up to be beautiful with a small nose, any lowlife might love me. This way, though, only the one would love me. Then he said, 'Look at yourselves! You are two ordinary, unattractive people and your noses have never concerned you!' My parents begged, 'But she could be so beautiful—we feel sorry for her!' but the sorcerer refused to do anything. And now I'm all grown up. I work as a hairdresser. I'm good at my job and there's a waitlist to see me. But I'm unhappy."

"There's nothing I can do," said the doctor. "Go to the next town over—a wizard lives there, maybe he can help you."

So Nina got on a train. She was seated in the same compartment as a young man in threadbare clothes. He was reading a thick book and paid no attention to her. That night, the train lurched and the sleeping Nina fell off the top bunk. She awoke in the young man's arms.

"You're lucky I was awake to catch you," he said.

"Thank you," said Nina, standing up. "You should come by my hair salon—it's the one in the main square— I'll give you a free haircut and shave."

"No, thank you. I cut my own hair and trim my beard with big sheep shears every six months."

"Then come by to have some tea."

"Thank you, but I prefer to drink tea alone," said the young man, opening his book.

"Then just come by."

"No, I can't do that. I'm busy."

By then, the train had arrived in the neighboring town and Nina went to see the wizard. He was a handsome young man with a black beard, wearing striking sunglasses. He told Nina that he could indeed help her, but as payment, he wanted her right thumb. Nina agreed and became incredibly beautiful—just down one thumb.

When she stepped out of the wizard's house, people stopped in their tracks, cars honked, and men rushed to escort her to the train station. On the train, she was offered a bottom bunk and gifted lemonade, bouquets of roses, and several boxes of chocolates. When she got back to her town, the same thing happened. And a count began following her around in his car. He lowered his window and begged her to marry him. But Nina didn't get into his car.

Now Nina spent her days wandering the town in hopes of finding the young man from the train. She could no longer work as a hairdresser since her right hand was missing its most important digit, but she still had a bit of money saved up, so all day long she would roam the streets. All the while, the count's car would follow her.

Every day Nina was invited to multiple balls. She was considered the most beautiful woman in the town (even in the world, according to some). But no one knew that she had run out of money and ate only one meal a day—coffee and ice cream at the ball. Eventually, she couldn't take it any longer, so she got a job as a cleaning woman, saved up some money, and went to see the wizard again.

"Take all my money," Nina said to the wizard. "Just please tell me where to find my beloved, the man from the train,"

"Okay," said the wizard. "Give me back your small nose and I'll tell you."

"No. Take anything you want, but not that."

"Fine. I'll have to take another finger—your right index finger this time."

"Okay," said Nina without hesitation.

"The man lives in your town. His address is 2 Right Hand Street, attic apartment. Hurry!"

Nina raced to the train station, returned to her town, and found the man's house. She went up to her beloved's attic apartment.

"Do you remember me?" she said.

"No," said the young man.

"You caught me when I fell from the top bunk on the train, remember?"

"No, that wasn't you. That girl had a completely different face. She was very funny-looking!" Nina didn't know what else to say, so she left. But she returned to Right Hand Street every day to look up at the young man's window.

Now Nina always wore gloves, only taking them off at night when she scrubbed stairwells. She was invited to more balls, birthday parties, and town celebrations. The count continued to follow her in his car, and every two weeks he would propose. But Nina always refused, saying, "Who knows what kind of person you really are? Right now you say you'll do anything for me, but what if you turn out to be jealous or greedy, or resent having to support me? Who knows . . ."

One night, after finishing her cleaning duties, Nina went to look at the young man's window and saw an old woman dressed in black drawing the curtains. Beside herself with fear, Nina ran up to the attic and rang the doorbell. The old woman in black answered.

"What do you want?"

"Tell me! What's wrong with him?" asked Nina.

"Who?"

"The young man who lives here. I don't know his name."

"And who are you?" asked the old woman.

"He saved me once, on a train," said Nina.

"Then come in. He's very sick."

Nina walked in and saw her beloved lying under a blanket, breathing heavily.

"Who are you?" he said with effort. "I don't know you—you're not who you say you are."

"What's happened to you?" asked Nina.

"I fell ill after studying in the library basement. I must've learned too much. But this doesn't concern you. I will die soon."

The old woman nodded.

Nina ran off, boarded a night train, and arrived at the wizard's door.

"There's nothing more I can do for you," said the wizard.

"I'm begging you!" Nina began to cry. "Save my beloved! Take whatever you want—take my right hand; I can wash floors with my left one."

"I want your small nose."

"Take it and save him."

And instantly she looked exactly like she had before.

When she stepped outside, not a single person even looked at her. No one stopped in their tracks and no one escorted her to the station. On the train, she wasn't gifted a single rose or box of chocolates. When she arrived in her town, she saw the count's car waiting by the station, but the count didn't recognize her, even though she was dressed in her usual gray dress, gray flats, and gray hat.

Nina sprinted to Right Hand Street, ran up to the attic, and walked straight into her beloved's apartment. He was sitting on his bed drinking a beer.

"Oh, it's you!" he exclaimed. "I'm glad to see you

again! Some girl came here claiming to be you. But that didn't fool me. You're the funniest-looking girl I've ever seen—you're hard to forget."

Nina laughed and cried at the same time. And the room seemed to fill with sunshine and falling pearls.

"Why are you crying?" asked the young man. "Would you like to marry me?"

"I'm not the same as I was when we met," said Nina and pulled the gray glove off of her right hand.

"That? That's nothing. My name is Anisim and I'm a doctor. I've read every book in the library. I read the very last one lying on the damp floor of the library's basement." Anisim reached toward a shelf filled with potions, medicine, and pill bottles. "Here, take this," he said, passing her a bottle.

Nina took a small spoonful of medicine and her right hand turned back to normal.

"I'm only restoring what was there before," said Anisim. "And nothing more."

And soon Nina married her beloved Anisim and bore him many funny-looking children.

THE PRINCE WITH GOLD HAIR

ONCE UPON A TIME THERE LIVED A prince with gold hair. Of course, he was born bald like most babies, and no one could've guessed that by his first birthday he would sprout golden curls. And when these curls appeared, the royal family was mortified: how in the world was the boy blond? All the royal annals and portraits of his father's family were consulted (his mother's family was not taken into account: she was a young queen from a far-away, run-down kingdom and, as is the way with these things, was brought over because of a portrait hailing her as the most beautiful woman in the world, and in the end nothing good came of it—as the ladies-in-waiting had long warned the king, "don't marry out of your league").

The point is: no blonds were found in the family. The only blond in the whole court was the king's personal courier, who had once brought a gift for the young queen from her husband while he was at war—a pound of oranges. The courier spent one day and one night at the palace, then returned to the front with a gift for the king—a coin purse woven out of the queen's own hair.

The blond courier never returned from the war—maybe he was killed, maybe something else. As for the king, he arrived from the battlefield soon after the oranges, and it would seem that his son was born at the right time. But now, when the boy was carried out to his guests on the occasion of his first birthday, it was discovered that the crown prince was blond, just like that courier!

To cut to the chase, no one tried to cover anything up; the ladies-in-waiting said their piece ("a leopard can't change its spots") and a new, bald courier showed up at the queen's doorstep and read her a stamped decree. At that moment, the queen was feeding the prince and was too preoccupied to understand a thing, but she soon found herself and her now-worthless son shoved out of the palace and the kingdom.

"They're lucky they weren't executed," said the ladies-in-waiting. The king was nowhere to be seen, so the young queen walked away from the kingdom gates and toward the mountains, beyond which lay the sea, beyond which was town N, the home of her elderly parents.

Night was falling and the infant's hair shone in the twilight because, in fact, it was pure gold. And with the aid of this dim light, the queen carried her son higher and higher into the mountains. When she grew tired, she found an empty cave, and that's where the mother and son fell asleep. That night, she had wild dreams of scurrying squirrels, or maybe rabbits, but was too exhausted to open her eyes. In the morning, while brushing her son's hair, she discovered that he was missing a big chunk—as if it had been roughly chopped off with a knife. The queen was a shrewd seventeen-year-old and caught on quick.

"If you took an ounce of gold from my son's head, at least give us something to eat!" she said to the empty cave. Just then, a rock fell out of the cave wall, and in the resulting hole she found a teeny bowl of hot pea soup with a tiny spoon. The queen thanked the cave squirrels and rabbits for the soup, then ate it up and nursed her son, and the two of them continued on their journey through the mountain passes toward the sea.

She didn't sleep in caves after that; now she slept in the daytime and traveled at night by the light of her son's gold hair. She was right to be cautious, else the invisible mountain dwellers may have shaved the boy bald, and all for just a bowl of soup in return! The queen ate berries and wild pears, which were plentiful along the mountain road. When they finally reached the sea, it was evening. They sat on the shore gazing into the blue expanse and listening to the crashing waves. The queen told her son that his grandparents were waiting for them on the opposite shore, while the boy's gold hair glowed brighter and brighter as the night grew dark. Naturally, the light attracted a fishing boat.

The fisherman gaped in awe at the glowing infant. He asked what the mother and child were doing there on the beach, and the queen told him they were waiting to catch a boat to town N. The fisherman offered to take them to the nearest town, A, which at least had a harbor where they could find such a boat, since "waiting for a boat here is like waiting for pigs to fly." The queen agreed and the fisherman rowed for two hours straight, never once taking his eyes off the boy. By midnight, by the light of the gold hair, the queen and her son were shown to the fisherman's hut and laid to sleep on a rug in the corner.

The next morning at daybreak, the fisherman burst into the police station yelling that he'd found an infant with a glow around his head, and that the boy and his mother should be arrested at once, otherwise it would be like last time—people would riot and proclaim that judgment day had come.

The fisherman wasn't wrong. Once before, a newcomer to the town had constructed himself a pair of wings and climbed to the top of a tower intending to fly. The townspeople mistook him for an angel heralding the final judgment. Quickly, before this judgment was to begin, the townspeople took their chance to air their grievances against the town judges, police force, and royal council.

And then, sobbing and crossing themselves, crawled on their knees toward the town hall. The fisherman was one of those rioting townspeople, hollering about his poor man's woes, and was sentenced to two years of hard labor during which he was reformed (because he was promised that next time, he'd be hanged alive). He also signed an oath, vowing to alert the police of future wing-sightings or anything else of the sort—and that's exactly what he was doing.

Meanwhile, the fisherman's mother, unaware of her son's nighttime adventures (the fisherman hadn't told her anything, wary of her loose lips), saw a beautiful young woman washing a blond infant at the water barrel in her yard and promptly kicked them out. She didn't want her son marrying some broad with a child: it was well known that bastard sons sometimes grew up to be bandits. She was a wise woman—her own son had grown up with a stepfather and had consequently been to prison.

Thus the queen and her son returned to the seashore and took shelter under an overhanging crag. They slept, the mother bathed her son in the surf, they played in the sand and searched for shells; they didn't have anything to eat but, in the evening, the infant glowed with a renewed vigor and his mother hid him under the crag so he wouldn't be seen from the town.

Still, a dinghy full of sailors came from the sea, drawn

to the shore as if to a lighthouse, and a gallant captain wearing a peaked cap approached the crag. He asked what the lovely mother and son were waiting for and offered his help—that is to say, the use of his ship—when he learned that they wanted to get to town N. As you may have guessed, the captain already knew that the town was being combed for the long-awaited judge in the form of an infant emitting an unearthly light. The police, army, air force, and navy were all called to action, and the captain himself was leading the search efforts from the direction of the sea. But when he saw the infant and his mother, he decided to take pity on them and not turn them in (after all, people are much smarter than we give them credit for, especially when it comes to matters of money). Knowing the loquacity of his rowers, the captain advised the mother to cover her son's head, then loaded the precious passengers onto the dinghy and rowed them out to his ship. Once aboard, the passengers were put in a comfortable cabin, assigned a sailor with a machine gun and a lackey who provided hot meals, and after a short trip they all arrived in the neighboring town B.

Next, the captain set off in full dress uniform, complete with insignia and dirk, to negotiate with a traveling circus. That very evening, a covered truck equipped with a secure cage arrived at the harbor, and a number of heavily armed sailors led the queen and her kerchiefed son down the gangplank to the truck and then locked up.

The queen didn't understand where they were, but—thanks to her son's habit of illuminating everything—she saw a pile of hay in the corner and a large bowl of water. The place smelled like a pigsty. The queen sat down on the hay with her son, the truck began moving, and so began a very bizarre life.

The caged mother and son were transferred to the circus's elephant house, where they were given one bowl of hot gruel twice a day. Every evening they were moved to a cage with wheels, a white sheet was draped over the queen's tattered clothes while the boy was undressed, and the two of them were transported down a corridor into the circus tent and right into the ring. Music played as if for mass (featuring an accordion), and a whisper ordered the queen to stand and hold the naked infant out toward the audience. Then all the lights would go out and the boy, as he was wont to do, would radiate light, illuminating his mother and parts of the cage, making the spectators sob and pull their children closer. Then the whole sideshow would be carted away until the next evening. The queen did everything she was told because she understood that if she objected, they'd simply hire a new mother—one more capable of following directions.

The food was disgusting—she was fed the same thing as the monkeys in the cage next door, though better than the elephant in the corner, who ate only hay. But the queen forced herself to eat the soggy bread crusts and boiled cabbage leaves because she was nursing her son and she had to keep it together! The boy captured the affections of everyone—the monkeys, the parrots, and even the elephant—and at night all was calm and jovial and the birds and animals looked happy and well-fed in the faint glow emanating from his hair. Actually, they looked that way in the ring, too, and the circus flourished, in large part because of its final act with the queen and her son.

But soon it came time to get out of town, because tales of the glowing infant spread and the circus began attracting the wrong kind of audiences—they paid no attention to the dancing monkeys or joking clowns; they never laughed or bought ice cream or even applauded. They came for one thing only: the queen and her son. When the pair was carted into the ring, the crowd would begin crying and chanting. (And what do you call thousands of people chanting at once? A nightmare for management, that's what!) There were processions of people on their knees trying to crawl straight into the ring. And the elephant house was frequently under siege from people shoving ill loved ones under its walls with cries of "Heal them!" The police stationed a guard, who soon grew rich charging people to kiss the walls of the elephant house. It quickly became the most coveted police post in town, and officers began rotating out every two hours on their own initiative, though the changing of the guard happened without any pomp because everyone just wanted their share—this wasn't the time for pageantry.

And when it was time for the circus to leave, management hired an armored vehicle and a troop of Blue Berets with automatic weapons. The circus director and the ship captain personally came to the elephant house to ask the queen which towns besides A and B she wished to visit. And did she have any friends or family in these towns?

The queen quickly put two and two together and conducted herself like a true double agent. She readily told them that her hometown was C and that she had acquaintances, friends, and relatives absolutely everywhere in D, E, and so on alphabetically, with the exception of town N, where all that was left were her grandparents' graves (which she'd been planning to visit when she met the captain). She was sure that the circus would be filled every night with all the people who knew and loved her and her son, but not in town N—in town N she couldn't promise anything of the sort. At that point the captain and director both nodded knowingly, as if struck with the same thought.

A few days later, at sunrise, the circus departed from its well-worn spot, leaving behind a throng of pilgrims sleeping by the (now closed) ticket office, trampled dirt, holes where the tent poles had been, and piles of garbage. The armored car, surrounded by mounted Blue Berets, as well as all the animal cages and a van full of performers were loaded onto a ship headed straight to town N. As the queen was being escorted off the ship, she was able to glimpse the beach under her feet despite the sheet over her head; it was covered in colorful stones—agates, amethysts, and black amber—and she knew that this could be only her beloved hometown N.

Her elderly forty-year-old parents lived here. They'd shed many a tear when an overseas king, threatening their flourishing kingdom with war and ruin, demanded that their daughter (touted as the most beautiful woman in the world) marry his son. And why not? This is the sort of thing royals busy themselves with—they try to improve and improve their bloodlines, with the aim of breeding the most beautiful, most intelligent children. To be fair, all of humanity is striving for this—every family wants to produce the finest, most valued offspring. But it was the king and queen of N who happened to produce such a daughter, and the militant neighboring royals decided that since luck wasn't on their side (their son was constantly brooding), there was only one way to improve their bloodline. But bad luck again—this time they were dealt a blond heir.

•

And so, the captive, beautiful queen was back to sitting in a cage, eating bread crusts and cabbage leaf soup while her son beamed gently, chattering to the parrots and monkeys in their animal language. This greatly amused the elephant keeper, a dark-haired, ungainly woman who laughed only when she saw someone slip and fall and break whatever they were holding—like a bottle or, better yet, a carton of eggs. She also laughed at fools, among whose ranks she'd placed the boy.

"That runt," she'd say, "is basically a monkey himself." This miserable woman spent her whole salary on wine. As for food, she'd pick the best pieces out of the animal feed and cook them up in a small pot over a fire every evening. She grumbled and cursed without end and only at the sight of the boy would she laugh, wagging her finger at him and sometimes even treating him to a carrot or a turnip from her stockpile. The elephant keeper's greatest dream was to be transferred to the tiger house, because she'd assumed that its keeper went home every night with a purse full of meat. She regularly complained to the circus director about the tiger keeper's thieving ways, but the tiger keeper had her own methods: she was friends with the director's secretary, who loved her children as any mother does and liked having access to meat with which to feed them.

Yes, such were the backstage dramas of the circus,

and every day the queen listened to the elephant keeper's complaining and cursing. The queen genuinely hated this woman even though the elephant keeper tried to justify herself with tragic tales of her husband, who'd disappeared and left her to raise three children, all of whom now expected her to bring them care packages in prison. The queen, who wasn't very grown but who'd already suffered much, couldn't stand thieves—even though she understood that people who stole only did so because they had no other option. And then these people had children. And then they had to steal for their children. And it is said that stealing for children is saintly. But back to the point.

The queen decided to plan her escape.

She understood that no one would ever recognize her in the circus ring. The director insisted that her face be powdered snow-white with chalk and her eyebrows be drawn on with soot—he thought it looked good, plus this "makeup" was cheap. And it's why no one in the world, not even the queen's own mother and father, would ever recognize her as that white, ghostly creature with harsh, black brows. Her only hope was the sole person who took care of her: the elephant keeper. One day, the keeper received this offer from the queen: enough money to last her the rest of her life—i.e., a pile a gold—if she would bring the queen a pencil and paper and then mail a letter for her.

The keeper agonized over the request; she even went to the director but, as usual, his secretary didn't let her in, so she decided to let the chips fall where they may. The keeper used her own money to buy paper, a pencil, and an envelope, then passed everything into the cage. That night, she dropped the letter into a mailbox and then, cursing everything in the world, began cooking a meatless cabbage soup and fantasizing about the ills that would one day befall the imperious director, his secretary, and the tiger keeper.

But what happened was something else entirely. First, the royal guard burst into the circus, promptly arrested the queen and her son, put them in a van labeled "Bread," and took off while the elephant keeper quite stupidly shrieked about the money she'd spent on the pencil and paper. And second, the elephant keeper was fired— no good deed goes unpunished, especially if the good deed is done without any pleasure.

Instead of being taken to the royal palace, as the queen had hoped, she and her son wound up in a windowless cell in a prison tower. The jailer on duty, out of sheer laziness, only brought them food on their second day, and when he walked into the cell with a flashlight and soup pot, he was shocked to find light already inside that black hole. The jailer set down the pot and gawked at the strange pair: the girl was wearing a white sheet and was as gaunt and transparent as a ghost—that, he'd seen before, but the baby with the glowing head blew his mind, especially since he was drunk.

"Don't be scared," the queen said to him. "Look— the boy's hair is pure gold. I'll give you some. If you have a knife, I'll cut you off a lock to prove it. You can take it to a jeweler and it'll fetch you a good sum."

Despite being drunk, the jailer knew not to trust the white-as-chalk girl with his knife, so he did it himself—he roughly hacked off a chunk of hair from the infant's head, shoved it in his pocket, and, swaying, walked out (without forgetting to lock the door). He spent that night at a pub drinking away all the money he'd gotten for the gold hair and the next morning returned to the prison absolutely livid. He barged into the queen's cell and chopped off all the boy's hair. The mother screamed and cried, so he cut off her long braid, too, and threw it on the ground.

"You think you'll be alive much longer?" he spat. "You'll be thrown in the lion pit tomorrow—you and your baby! You think you're here by mistake? No! The duchess herself wants you both dead! Her son, the king's second cousin once removed, is the sole heir to the throne and your parents, the king and queen, are ill—the prison doctor gives them medicine that makes them age a year in a single day. Tomorrow you'll be fed to the lion, and I'm not letting this gold to go to waste. I'm a poor student, I go to night school, and I have to work this backbreaking job just to make ends meet. Can you imagine living on a single salary—in this day and age? A word to the wise: don't write letters to kings. They're not the ones who read them!"

"If you're a student, then use your brain!" said the queen. "You just found a goldmine for life! You saw yourself—the boy's hair is pure gold!"

"Fine. I won't let them execute the boy. I'll put him on a chain in my basement and pick any random kid off the street to pass off as yours! Wouldn't be the first time," slurred the jailer.

"That won't work. My son lives on breast milk— that's how he gets his gold hair. Don't you get it, idiot? We're royalty!"

"You'll pay for calling me an idiot," said the jailer, swaying. "I'm just a law student now, but one day I'll be a court judge. Oh, you're a big shot alright—there are rumors about you up and down the coast. There's a big uprising planned in your defense, supposedly for all the country's suffering people, but the person in charge is just another student, like me. Who knows, maybe the revolutionaries will win and instead of the duchess's son, the bald student leader will be king; they can dig up your bones from the lion's pit, and all the other bones, too, and build a memorial . . ." The jailer staggered, waving his arms wildly, and suddenly his flashlight flew out of his hand, clattered to the floor, and went out. At once it was pitch-black. Even the boy dimmed, he glowed as faintly as a distant constellation in the Milky Way. The jailer fumbled around on the ground, searching for the flashlight, mumbled something, then lay down and quickly began snoring.

The queen grabbed her son, retrieved a handful of his gold curls from the jailer's pocket, and walked out into the prison hall. Random people wandered past her, not noticing her or one another, and all the guards were asleep—maybe it was a holiday or maybe this was normal in town N, where the king and queen no longer ruled and the duchess and her son did not yet reign. The prison gate was ajar, and the queen walked right out into the town square. It was the middle of the night. A single star hung in the sky, small but extremely bright, like the obstruction light on the end of a tower crane's jib. Unsurprisingly, the queen headed toward the sea. The star followed her, as stars do (stars always accompany people wherever it is they are going). Along the way they met a small procession: two soused soldiers were leading an elderly man and woman in the direction of the prison. In the light of the star, the queen immediately recognized the man and woman—they were her parents. Her father and mother looked like two shadows, frail and mute. They were holding hands. The queen approached the soldiers confidently.

"Hey, fellas, want a drink?"

The soldiers stopped but didn't say anything. Her parents stood shivering.

"You look like you need a break," continued the queen. "Go to the pub and I'll watch over these two."

"Don't have any money," said one soldier hoarsely, while the other coughed.

"No problem. Here's some pure gold. Go." She handed them a lock of gold hair from her pocket. Suddenly everything was illuminated. Or maybe it was just the star. The soldiers exchanged looks, spat on the ground, took the gold, and, tripping over themselves, ran to the pub.

"Mama, Papa, it's me, your daughter, and this is my son," said the queen. "I've returned for you. Let's get out of here."

They headed toward the sea and the star followed. Her parents didn't say a word; their eyes were open wide, but they walked as if in a trance. Surely, this was an effect of the prison "medications" they'd been given. When they reached the shore, the young queen knocked on the door of a fisherman's hut. She asked the man who answered if they could spend the night and promised to pay in the morning. A yawning woman took them to a barn and pointed to a pile of hay.

The boy awoke at sunrise. In the barn there were sheep sleeping in a pile, a cow, a horse chewing hay, and a few stray chickens. The boy spoke to the animals in the language he'd learned at the circus—the language of elephants, parrots, and monkeys—and all the barn animals stopped chewing and bowed deeply. The young queen left her son to converse with the animals in the company of her sleeping parents (who continued to hold hands) and ran to the bank. She exchanged one strand of gold hair for a heap of small coins and then bought some bread, cheese, and milk—what a blessing it was to run errands for the first time in her life and know that her son wasn't all alone! The queen had never before been as happy or as free as she was that morning. Roses bloomed all around, waves crashed in the distance, she was in her hometown, and her family was someplace safe—albeit a barn, but better that than a cave, an elephant house, or a prison cell. The queen had long forgotten the time when she'd had a hundred rooms and fifty servants. As she walked toward her safe haven, she noticed people staring after her—she figured there was a notice about her escape from prison and that, probably, they'd all soon be caught. So she quickly bought more food (apples, some eggs, and a basket of tomatoes) and returned to the barn. She paid the fisherman's wife and told her they were waiting to leave on a boat any day now. She didn't leave the property again.

She gingerly nursed her parents back to health with

food and milk, and the boy grew to love sitting on his grandfather's lap and playing with his long beard—grown out during his treatment at the prison hospital. (Since the king and queen were expected to die soon, they hadn't been given any food or towels, no razor for the king or comb for the queen; they were given only medication.)

Meanwhile, governance of the town had devolved into a complete free-for-all: various factions were fighting for control of the royal palace, the prison had its doors either flung open or its cells chock-full and locked, and the townspeople no longer worked, instead stockpiling weapons and ambling drunkenly down the streets, shooting into the air at random. The queen learned all this from the fisherman and his wife, who were terrified by all the explosions. Two of their windows had already been shattered, though it could've been worse, they told her—their cow and horse could've been stolen!

One day, the fisherman's wife came by the barn more upset than ever. She reported that the townspeople were convinced the world was ending because a single star hung in the sky day and night, always in the same spot, growing brighter by the hour as if descending to the earth. The young queen and her family continued to confine themselves to the barn and the yard. Little by little her parents grew healthier, though they still didn't speak or appear to understand what was happening to king took place in the nursery—his grandfather made the crown out of cardboard and decorated it with a silver chocolate wrapper. And the silver gleamed in the young king's gold hair.

QUEEN LIR

ONCE UPON A TIME IN A CERTAIN kingdom, an elderly queen whom everyone called Lir went a bit off her rocker, took off her crown, handed it over to her son, Kordel, and decided to finally take a vacation—in some backwoods place free of all modern conveniences at that.

Only simple-minded, rags-to-riches types build luxurious palaces; true aristocrats prefer an au naturel way of life, though their obligations don't allow them to trade their palaces for huts, shacks, or sheds. But our queen was a strong, independent woman and determined to do as she pleased. So, she set to work building herself a house down the road from the royal palace, constructed out of eighty unopened cardboard pasta boxes held together with tape. She achieved remarkable results: by nightfall her hut was ready.

Lir then flagged down a huge garbage truck on its way out of the palace grounds and ordered the driver to dump out all its contents right where it stood. The queen dug around in the resulting pile, gutted some trash bags, and found a stack of newspapers, which she used to cover the floor of her hut (you didn't expect her to sleep on the ground, did you?).

Meanwhile, back at the palace, every gardener on the payroll was called by walkie-talkie to reload all that Lir hadn't found useful back into the garbage truck, causing quite a fuss as they gathered banana peels, tiny bits of eggshell, and so on. Word got around that the queen was also determined not to use anything she'd been gifted or had previously owned. She would procure her food and anything else she might need on her own, by the sweat of her brow. When her son, King Kordel, heard this, he went down to the queen's hut to give her some sort of plastic card.

"Mother, this is a magic card," he said. "If you insert it into the slot of a little box near any bank, money will pop out. This way you can—of your own free will and with your own two hands—buy whatever you may need."

"I don't intend to take anything from you," said the queen, rejecting the card. She no longer wished to live off the money of her subjects, she told him. She'd simply find sustenance on her own, even if it meant going through the trash (she considered this more honest). Kordel turned red, disappeared, and in no time the whole palace staff was running around filling up a new garbage truck. They tossed in a mattress, two pillows, sheets, a camel hair blanket (a gift from a Mongolian soldier a hundred years ago—finally they'd found a use for it), a few buckets (borrowed from the chambermaids), and a pot, but then they began to worry—if Lir decided to cook some soup inside her pasta wigwam, would she, along with her hut, *become* the soup? So, they fished the pot out of the truck and instead threw in some prepackaged breads, jams, sausages, cheeses, watermelons, and eggs, then added some scraps of newspaper for authenticity, and sent the truck on its way.

Soon the garbage truck honked at Lir's cardboard stoop and generously dumped the entire, overflowing trash delivery right onto the ground. The queen began happily extracting food from under the mattress and pillows (you see, the food wound up buried beneath the linens because the lackeys hadn't thought about the mechanics of the dump: what went in the truck last, came out first, and what went in first, came out last—take note for the future). Lir laboriously burrowed under the mattress and began picking out sausages, cheeses, jams, and breads; her excitement knew no bounds. What's more, her favorite great-granddaughter, Princess Alice, rushed down from the palace to help. The two of them had a ball digging through the trash and were very surprised how many useful and delicious things were thrown out at the palace. "But that no longer concerns me," said the queen,

layer of newspapers. With a sigh of exhaustion, Lir settled down for the night: she snuggled under yet another newspaper, and, feeling quite warm and cozy, fell asleep.

In the morning, the queen did some calisthenics—another novel activity—then decided to wash up (And if I don't undress, my clothes will be washed too, thought the practical queen). But in her haste she accidentally dumped the wrong bucket all over herself, after which she grabbed the correct bucket and doused herself once more, and then used her pillow to mop up the floor. As it turned out, the queen didn't like living in such filth—there were crumbs, food scraps, and wet spots all over—so she headed outdoors.

That's when Lir saw something on the lawn that she must have missed in the previous day's garbage: a tray with a silver pot of steaming coffee, some rolls with jam, and a pot of oatmeal. There was also a plate, a teacup, and some silver spoons. The garbage man must've returned once he'd noticed her oversight and left everything on the lawn. What an upstanding man, thought the queen, attacking the food. Then she noticed the magic card right next to the coffeepot. Kordel must've thrown it out in frustration, and now it belonged to no one—it was trash. So Lir tucked the card into her pocket, in case of emergency. Finally, being the tidy woman that she was, the queen put her dirty silverware straight in the trash and decided that, from then on, she'd always throw out her used dishes herself.

With that, Lir walked through the palace gates and off its grounds. The royal gatekeepers stood frozen, not knowing what to do. They were on strict orders not to let anyone in, but they'd been told nothing about letting people out, unless they were carrying something. Otherwise, people were free to leave as they wished. Needless to say, they hadn't recognized the queen in such a state (wearing a drenched, stained dress and without a hat—she'd thrown it out, but more about that later). So for the first time in her life, Lir charged down the street all by herself. Actually, a detachment of armed guards—the ones who'd been hiding in the bushes—immediately rushed after her, but by then the gatekeepers had come to their senses and stopped them, demanding permits for carrying out weaponry. Letting out an empty-handed granny was one thing, but the armed guards were in possession of all kinds of palace property: uniforms, flags, pants, boots, footwraps, sabers, swords, handkerchiefs, spears, etc.

As the queen strutted solo down the street sans hat, she saw from her reflection in a store window that her hair was a mess. As for how the queen came to be bareheaded, well, she'd used her soaking wet hat to sweep the floor, then had no choice but to throw it out in that *other* bucket. She'd remembered how the royal guards would remove their feathered hats, bow down, and swiftly dust the palace floor with the feathers, so she had tried to sweep her hut in the same way. But her hat had promptly split in two, unable to handle such a workload—so into the bucket it went!

Think about it: the royal quarters were always cleaned when the queen was away, so Lir remained quite clueless. She'd never laid eyes on a broom or dustpan in all her life. Apparently, the poor woman imagined that chambermaids swept with hats. (Come to think of it, many men and children wish it were that way in their homes; they don't want to see any of the process, just the results. But, like it or not, they end up witnessing it all—the laundry, the ironing, the sweeping, the potato peeling, the pasta boiling—and are sometimes even obliged to help out. Alas, not everyone can be a queen!)

Normally, Lir got her hair brushed twice a day—once in the morning and again before the evening ball. By this point, though, it had been more than twenty-four hours since her last brushing. Even if the queen had bought a hairbrush, she wouldn't know what to do with it—she hadn't the skill to stick it in her mane and drag it down in the direction of her feet, ruthlessly yanking out everything that obstructed its path. After all, grooming is an art.

The disheveled queen raced down the street, looking as ruffled as a feather duster, when suddenly in one of the shop windows, she spotted a man in a white smock laboring over a woman's curls. Her hair was covered in foam, like an ocean wave. Lir halted, walked into the hair salon, and sat down in a chair.

"Dearie, I'm ready," announced Lir.

A hairdresser went up the queen.

"Would you like a haircut?"

"I would." Lir was always very agreeable and never argued with her servants.

"How would you like it?" asked the pestilent hairdresser.

"Like that," said Lir, pointing to a photo on the wall. The photo (an advertisement for hair dye) depicted a young man shaved bald except for a strip of hair going down the center of his scalp—not unlike a horse's mane. The strip of hair was green. Maybe Lir wanted to become unrecognizable, so no one would point at her and chant things like, "Queen of hearts, go eat some tarts!" Or maybe she wanted to try something she'd never be able to get away with as queen. But most likely, she just hadn't gotten a good look at the photo—after all, her glasses were back at the palace.

"Like that?!" asked the hairdresser, double-checking.

"Yes," confirmed Lir. She couldn't stand

back-and-forth with lackeys—servants ought to know their place

The hairdresser did as he was told without another moment's hesitation, and Lir paraded out of the salon clean-shaven with a three-inch-tall green mohawk. The hairdresser was in such a state of shock at his own handiwork that he forgot all about the payment. The queen hadn't remembered either, since she'd never paid for anything in her life—couldn't even imagine such a thing. Outside, a gawking cyclist rammed into a pole, taxi drivers honked, school children whistled, and old women applauded—Lir was quite the spectacle.

But the commotion on the street was nothing new to her; Lir was always greeted with honking, applause, whistling, and swarming. Normally, she was quickly whisked away from such throngs, but this time she had to escape on her own. So she hopped onto the first vehicle she saw—a red Harley-Davidson racing motorcycle—and drove off. (One of the queen's adolescent mistakes was a young special forces officer with a motorbike. He'd let her drive it around at dawn. Ah, life back then was filled with hopes and dreams . . . and meddling ladies-in-waiting.)

The key had been sticking out of the ignition because the motorcycle belonged to the town's most infamous thief, Ferdinand, who never worried about his possessions as he was certain he was the only bad guy around and assumed everyone else was an honest citizen. (He'd erroneously gotten this idea in the first grade, and it drove poor Ferdinand to drop out, not wanting to be the worst in his class—can you blame him? Though when it came to thieves, he was certainly the best.)

Lir sped down the street on the stolen motorcycle, ignoring every traffic law (she wasn't aware they existed). But it all ended rather quickly: the cool biker (green mohawk, soiled blue dress, wet shoes) noticed a police officer in the distance and slammed on the brakes. Luckily, she'd noticed him from afar—old people are as farsighted as hawks—and by the time the officer got to the bike, Lir had already disappeared into the nearest store.

The officer was already suspicious when he saw Ferdinand's bike outside of the thief's usual neighborhood—thieves and police have strictly divided spheres of influence within every city—and once he noticed that its driver was a green-haired stranger, his suspicion grew. Ferdinand never gave anything to anyone, least of all his bike. Could this be a theft?

And thus began the manhunt for Queen Lir.

Meanwhile, inside the store, Lir found herself quite an outfit: a leather jacket covered in studs, thigh-high suede boots (just like her great-grandfather's hunting boots), and a pair of white jeans. She quickly changed in front of a mirror, tossing her dress and shoes on the floor, then grabbed sunglasses and a gray wig on her way out. Lir exited the store unimpeded and without paying (for the same reason as previously mentioned), while the shopkeeper went on arranging things in the back of the store, oblivious to the fact that he had been robbed.

The queen walked down the street in her new outfit, enjoying her freedom (the police officer was standing by the motorcycle awaiting orders from his superior and didn't recognize Lir in the slightest). Everything was going great, but it was about time for her second breakfast, and the queen's stomach growled like a stalled truck. The queen couldn't make sense of these noises—her body had never produced such growls before—but as soon as she came across a food stall, she found herself being dragged toward its rolls and sausages as if by an invisible lasso.

"Ma'am?" asked the vendor, and a minute later, Lir was sinking her porcelain teeth into a foot-long sandwich with the fervor of a feral cat. For comfort's sake, Lir tore off her sunglasses and wig, and the vendor, seeing Lir's shaved head and green mohawk (like a thick row of freshly sprouted dill), froze in shock with his arm outstretched (for obvious reasons). Soon, people began flocking to the food stall, attracted no doubt by the green-haired granny, but since it was considered rude in this kingdom to loiter around for no reason, they all lined up to buy sandwiches (while stealing surreptitious looks at Lir), and the vendor was forced to move on. Lir, having eaten half of her sandwich, returned the uneaten half to the vendor with the words, "Thank you, dearie. You can take this away now." She always spoke this way to her servants. For some reason, the vendor felt compelled to bow down in response—but then quickly pretended he was just tying his shoe. He was embarrassed for bowing, and yet, it also felt right—he was filled with a sense of duty and decided that the money didn't matter.

Now that she was sated, the liberated queen thought of Princess Alice; the child languished in the castle under strict watch while an incredibly vibrant life brewed right outside. I ought to summon her by phone, thought the queen, though she'd never actually dialed a phone herself—others did that for her. She paused in thought amid the mass of chewing, ogling people, then sighed, put on her wig and sunglasses, and dove into the nearest store—shopping really suited her!

The store happened to sell all the newest gadgets, from computers to phones, which was convenient since a phone was exactly what Lir needed. Once again, the salesclerk was nowhere to be found. Lir wandered the aisles, twisting knobs and flipping switches, when suddenly, an agonizing wail rang out. The clerk appeared out of nowhere, mouth full of food, and turned off whatever it was that Lir had turned on. In the resulting silence, the queen turned to him.

"Dearie, fetch me a phone," she said.

"What kind of phone would you like?" asked the clerk, wiping his mouth with a napkin.

"A phone that can make calls," said Lir sweetly. The clerk realized that before him was a rare idiot (who would think to ask for a phone that couldn't make calls?) and knew this type of customer could, and should, be duped. The young clerk was up to the task.

"A phone that can make calls?"

"Yes, a phone that can call the palace."

"One moment, ma'am, we've got a phone that can do just that," said the clerk, disappearing. Lir ended up waiting for quite some time, but the queen's upbringing didn't allow her to lose her temper. She spent the next half hour as if she were a soldier on duty, standing erect and smiling cordially. She stood like this on a daily basis, awaiting the end of the cavalry procession and the start of the marching band, or the end of everyone's speeches and the signal that it was time for her to cut the ribbon with those silver scissors. All the while, the clerk was searching for the phone number of the palace. If he could find it, he could sell any old phone to the clueless granny for an exorbitant price, claiming it was the only phone that could call the palace. It so happened that in this kingdom there were some dishonest salespeople who were eager to charge high prices for cheap goods. Finally, through his cousin who always bragged about being married to the son of a delivery man for the parliament's caterer, the clerk procured the palace phone number. (In return, he promised to sell his cousin's old computer for the price of a new one.) He reappeared, sweaty from all the negotiations.

"Ma'am, this is the phone that can call the palace. Here you go!" And the clerk ceremoniously dialed the number.

"Hello?" said the queen meekly. "Is this William? Dearie, connect me to Princess Alice. Thank you. Hello, who is this? Brunhilda? Put Alice on. It's fine—she's got school every day. Can you hear me? BRUNHILDA? Hello? Oh, it's you! Alice, it's me! It's great out here—come join me. Inform me of your address," she said, turning to the clerk. "Right. I'm at 10 Sweet Bun Street. But don't say a word to anyone! Walk out of the palace, take a right, then a left and you'll find me."

Lir spent the next ten minutes politely listening to the clerk, who was sure he'd convinced her to buy a pedal-operated phone, a device for angling fish in shallow waters, a bamboo mower, night-vision goggles for the theater, a remote-controlled appetite stimulator, and an in-home manure converter; at the eleventh minute, Sweet Bun

Street erupted with sirens and a company of motorized infantry burst into the store.

But the clever Lir had heard the approaching sirens and slipped away to the opposite side of the street, removing her wig and sunglasses as she went. She hid out in another store, watching from its window the ensuing invasion of police, journalists, and cameramen. Alice had arrived in a black stretch-limo the size of a volleyball court, accompanied by two young ladies-in-waiting, Brunhilda and Cunegonde, who'd only been at the palace for the past forty-five years. The two women dashed into the store, each scrambling to be first to grab the queen, while Alice lagged behind. Lir pounced at this opportunity, yelling from her side of the street, "Alice! Cuckoo!"

Alice turned around—"cuckoo" was their battle cry whenever they played hide-and-seek in the royal bedchamber—and calmly crossed the street, weaving between motorcycles, armored vehicles, and police buses. Lir motioned Alice into the store, where there was not another soul to be found. The queen had learned by then that salesclerks were the rarest and laziest species in this city jungle. The customer had to attract this animal by yelling, lure it to the counter, and force it to take money. Alice and the queen watched with interest as the street filled with people, a helicopter squadron flew in, and a pack of search and rescue hounds arrived. Any available free space was quickly consumed by television crews, including the small store where Lir and her great-grand-daughter were hiding.

One cameraman had the nerve to ask Alice to hold a cable and then handed a big, heavy case to Lir. When the police peeked into the store, they mistook Lir and Alice for a small camera crew because, at that moment, the producer was screaming at them, reproaching Lir for shattering a piece of equipment into a million pieces. (You see, Alice had gotten bored of holding the cable, so she dropped it on the ground. Lir tried to step over it, but it caught on her heel, and you can guess what happened next. The case itself lay on the floor unharmed, but when the cameraman picked it up, it jangled melodiously—just like the old grandfather clock at the palace.)

"Where's the jack plug, ladies?" screamed the cameraman. "Where'd it go? Give me the jack plug, morons!"

Upon hearing such name-calling, the police tactfully departed. Lir, on the other hand, wasn't the least bit offended, as she'd never heard the word "moron" before. Unperturbed, she turned to Alice.

"Darling, I think they've lost some jack plug morons, if I'm not mistaken," she said.

"But I don't think I have them, if I'm not mistaken!" said Alice.

"How could it have gone AWOL?" screamed the cameraman.

"Alice, dear, did you happen to put them in a wall?" Lir asked her great-granddaughter, to which the girl shook her head.

"If I'm not mistaken, my dear friend," said Lir politely to the cameraman, "Alice didn't put your jack plug morons in a wall. I suggest you look elsewhere, dear."

Hearing all the commotion, a weary salesclerk finally emerged.

"Dearie," the queen addressed her, "we need to find a way out of here—the place is simply crawling with police." The clerk silently turned and walked off and the royal duo followed, eventually exiting through a back door onto the adjacent street, Wading Cow Avenue. By the look on her face, it seemed the clerk desperately wanted to go with them, but ultimately she forced herself to return to her workplace.

Lir and Alice strolled along Wading Cow Avenue, people-watching and window-shopping. They went into three more stores, each time changing into new outfits without anyone stopping them. Remember, this kingdom had a limited number of thieves—just Ferdinand and a handful of others. And Ferdinand was currently at the police station filing a report for a stolen motorcycle. The queen and her great-granddaughter wandered around the city for hours—what could be better than a leisurely day of shopping? (And, lest you worry, the wise queen transferred her son's magical card into the pocket of every new outfit she put on.)

By six o'clock, Alice was dressed in a sailor's shirt and leather pants, parading around in six-inch heels and carrying a laughing baby doll—when her belly was pushed, the doll exploded in a fit of hysterical laughter with notes of fear and anguish. Alice delighted in the terrifying laughter—she'd never heard anything like it at the palace—so she pushed the doll's belly over and over. Lir had donned a fetching red suit that she would never have dared to wear before. It was bedecked in gold details, with a plunging neckline and a mini skirt to boot. Lir felt like a naive lass, especially when she accessorized with a curly blond wig, sunglasses, and a cowboy hat. The wig's curls hung over her face and neck, covering them entirely (a magical feeling!), and the queen strutted down the street in her suede boots like a young ballerina next to a teetering Princess Alice the Fourteenth holding a maniacal baby doll—the pair were quite the marvel!

As they left yet another store without paying, a wailing sound rang out—it was the security alarm. But the guard didn't even budge (if he had left his post, chased after the thieves, caught them, and brought them to the station, other thieves would've cleaned out the whole store while he was so occupied). This was a clever, well-known tactic, and the guard watched the women with a knowing smile. The one with curly hair was practically screeching with laughter, although she acted like she was doing nothing of the sort, while her companion tormented a baby doll with gusto. But the guard did raise his baton and shake it menacingly at them, which frightened Lir terribly.

"Run, Alice, we've been recognized! He's giving us the royal salute with his staff!" They took off down Wading Cow Avenue, pushing people out of their way with cries of "Excuse me, dearie" and "My apologies, dear," and slowed down only after about a mile. By this point, the day had turned to evening. Lir's stomach began to growl again—like a car engine struggling to warm up on a cold day—while Alice's squeaked and whined. Naturally, they approached a pie vendor.

This particular vendor was penniless and inexperienced. It was his first day on the job—his wife had baked some crappy pies and shoved him out the door to sell them, adding, "Don't come home with less than a thousand!" The pies were filled with boiled apple peels and the outer leaves of cabbage, which are normally thrown away, so the pie man had come to consider himself a dishonest man. And it's a well-known fact that when someone has no self-respect, they don't treat others with much respect either. In short, the pie man assumed the worst of everyone.

"Pies! Pies with organic fillings!" he yelled aggressively. "Not a gram of sugar" (this was true), "not a drop of fat" (also true), "made of coarse-meal flour" (i.e., cattle feed). People rushing home from work bought the pies but shied away from eating them on the go and instead took them home. (In this kingdom it was considered rude to eat in public—what if a hungry passerby was offended by your loud chewing? Hungry people can be quite dangerous.) So the cheated customers hurried away none the wiser, while the queen and princess took the man's last two "cabbage" pies and immediately began devouring them.

"Hey," said the pie man. "What about my money, ladies?"

"Alice, do these pies remind you of . . . what's that material pots are made out of? I think it's called damp clay?"

"No way," said the man angrily. "Pay up!"

"I'm afraid you're right, Grandma," said Alice, pulling out a sopping piece of twine that had made its way into the pie along with the cabbage.

"Dearie, I'm afraid I'm going to have to return this," said Lir, laboriously peeling away a piece of raw dough from her costly porcelain teeth. "Take it. Feel free to eat it yourself."

Alice simply spat the twine-filled pie on the ground.

"I'm calling the police!" screamed the pie man.

"Yes, good idea," said Lir, extracting lodged pieces of dough from her teeth with her pinky (and why not—she wasn't at the palace). "The police ought to handle this."

The pie man rushed to the nearest pay phone but didn't account for one thing—the two women were unaware of their own kingdom's customs, i.e., that once the police were called you were supposed to remain at the spot of the crime. So as soon as the pie man had shut himself inside the phone booth, our two adventurers ran off, disappearing into the fog of Wading Cow Avenue.

It took the police an hour to arrive (remember, the entire police force was searching for Lir at 10 Sweet Bun Street), and by that time the pie man had already gotten a beating from his wife, who'd come to check on him and discovered he was short two pies' worth of money. He was angry, humiliated, and sporting a black eye and immediately told the police that he'd been attacked and robbed by two working women—a young one with curly blond hair, wearing a red skirt (he hadn't been able to see her face), and a very short one, wearing a sailor's outfit and high heels, laughing uncontrollably.

"Aha! We've just received a call from a fur store that a couple of thieves left behind a red skirt-suit and a pair of leather pants with a sailor's shirt," said the officer. "Did they leave any evidence here?"

"There's your evidence," said the pie man, pointing at the ground. "They spat out my pie!" The police immediately gathered the evidentiary material off the ground, grabbed the pie man as a witness, and raced to the fur store.

But Lir and Alice had long since left the fur store and, after a quick visit to an all-male cabaret, decided to take a little break from their adventures and were now sitting in a pub (they'd simply walked into the first establishment they came across). They told the waiter they were very thirsty, and he brought over two mugs of beer. (What else would you expect from a pub waiter? One must really be mindful of one's environment!) Of course, neither of them had ever been served beer at the palace, so from that point on everything got a bit more complicated.

The queen and her great-granddaughter pounced on the beer, crinkling their noses in unison when it hit their tongues. But they didn't want to insult the waiter with complaints such as "This lemonade is a bit bitter, don't you think, dearie?" Additionally, Alice ordered "that thing over there," and Lir chimed in with "Yes, one for me too, dearie," and the waiter brought over two sausages. The women bravely gulped from their mugs, ate the sausages, then ordered "another round of those things!" The waiter kept turning around on his way to the kitchen (who could blame him—his patrons appeared to be two

Japanese women wearing kimonos with black, almost lacquered hair, but both of them had blue eyes).

"Another order of sausages," he told the kitchen. "Those Japanese women have no idea that these are called sausages, but they speak our language fluently, and they're so polite, always calling me 'dearie.'"

"Japanese women?" asked the chef.

"Yes, but their eyes are blue! Have you ever seen such a thing?"

"They're just wearing contacts," said the chef knowingly.

"You're probably right—I hadn't thought of that."

By the time he brought over the second order of "those things," the two women were sitting with their heads drooping and their shoulders slumped. They tried to eat their sausages without much success; they kept missing their mouths and eventually gave up. Lir, being very practical, put her half-eaten sausage in her pocket for later.

This happened near the end of their adventures, but earlier Lir and Alice had wandered into a shop called *Furs for Newlyweds*, where they'd changed into luxurious fur coats, after which they popped into the male cabaret. The show du jour was *Women's Dances from Around the World*. The queen and princess had accidentally entered through the stage door and ended up backstage, right by a rack of costumes. Our two adventurers took such a liking to the colorful kimonos and black wigs hanging on the end of the rack that they immediately changed into them, abandoning their furs on the ground—a silver fox-fur coat and a pink flamingo-down jacket. The wardrobe department promptly stashed away the furs and didn't bother reporting the missing cheap kimonos and wigs to the police. So the furs, kimonos, and wigs went unaccounted for.

Thus when the police chief came on the evening news, it was with erroneous information: two thieves were wreaking havoc on Wading Cow Avenue dressed in expensive furs (one fox and one flamingo). Clearly these were the doings of an experienced gang, group of warrior women, or, worse still, the Russian Mafia. Their crimes included motorcycle larceny; shoplifting a leather jacket, white jeans, gray wig, boots, and sunglasses; shoplifting a sailor's shirt, leather pants, red suit, cowboy hat, and curly blond wig; as well as the theft of two twine-filled pies (investigators had analyzed the evidence), two fur coats, and one baby doll.

"A record number of crimes," said the police chief, "which carry a punishment of life in prison, plus forty-five years in exile, and the revocation of the perpetrators' driver's licenses."

The waiter, who managed to both serve his tables

and keep an eye on the TV, turned to the Japanese women (whose eyes were almost closed by this point) and asked, "Do you have thieves in Japan?"

"Pardon me?" Lir was overwhelmed by the beer and shocked by the news report—were she and Alice the "thieves" the police were looking for?

"In our kingdom, we clearly have a problem with thieves," said the waiter.

"I don't think I understand you," Lir cut him off. "We'd like two more of those things, please. Our audience has concluded. Off you go, dearie."

"Of course, madam," exclaimed the waiter, bowing. "For you, anything."

Before long, the waiter had to fulfill this promise because the two Japanese women had fallen asleep at the table and he was obliged to order them a taxi and escort them to the two-star motel where the pub's wobbliest guests often spent the night. In the morning, these guests were handed a bill (beer, taxi, motel room, broken mirror, doctor's visit, bandages—for them, for the doctor, for the night watchman—around-the-clock supervision by armed military personnel, etc.). The waiter was sure the women were good for the money—he'd seen the corner of a credit card peeking out of the granny's kimono pocket, so he took it upon himself to escort his patrons to the motel and managed to get them the best room.

•

The next morning, Lir awoke in a very strange place: there were no gilded mirrors, no canopy over the bed, and instead of a Persian rug there was some sort of balding, threadbare rag. And where are the sleeping ladies-in-waiting, the servants, and the orchestra? Her head felt heavy, though certainly not from her crown, and her mouth tasted like an unwashed iron fork (the queen had once used such a fork while visiting the shack of a pauper on the island of Tururoa; this pauper was the local czar). Poor Alice was asleep on the other bed in her kimono, wig, and heels.

My god! thought Lir. We're in prison! Suddenly, the previous day's events rushed back to her, and she understood that she and Alice had been sentenced to life in prison.

"Alice, wake up!" yelped Lir, her voice as sharp and harsh as the pauper's fork. "We've been arrested!"

There was a rough knock on the door.

"Alice, do you think they've come to execute us?" continued Lir. "Get up! We shall greet them with dignity and stoicism! Executions are always at dawn—and look, it's just that time, 11 a.m."

"Grandma," moaned Alice, "I don't want to get up at the crack of dawn. Can't they execute me in bed?"

A woman with a vacuum opened the door.

"May I?" she asked.

"I was not informed you were coming," said Lir.

"I'm here to clean the room."

"Go ahead, dearie. Chop chop."

The woman nodded, turned on her vacuum, and began racing around the jail cell, roaring and clamoring. When she disappeared into the bathroom and began splashing and scrubbing, Lir yelped, "We've got to make a run for it! She forgot to lock the cell door!" They dashed out into the corridor and began running, finally finding the stairs and descending in a flurry straight to the motel's glass doors.

"Hold it!" yelled the receptionist. "Hold it right there!" He was yelling because the guests hadn't paid for their stay or for any broken mirrors (the receptionist was in the middle of concocting a tally of how much furniture had been damaged and how many towels ripped and adding it all to their bill). But Lir and Alice darted out of the motel and leapt onto a departing bus.

The bus driver saw two rosy-cheeked Japanese women in his rearview mirror and expected them to come to the front to buy a ticket (in this kingdom bus tickets were purchased from the driver). And the women did walk up to him, breathing heavily.

"Hello, dearie. Do inform me where the palace is," said the older one in perfect local dialect.

"The palace?" asked the young driver. "The Palace of Sports?"

"If I'm not mistaken, that's not the one."

"Oh, maybe the Wedding Palace?"

"No, I don't think so."

"Maybe, the Palace of Culture named after Pierre the Great?"

"No, no, dearie. I need the royal palace."

"Oh, the Western Royal Palace?"

"Indeed, that's the one."

"What's going on there?" asked the driver.

"Nothing special. But could you take us there, darling? Entrance fourteen. You will not regret it, my dear."

"Entrance fourteen isn't on my route," said the driver, laughing heartily.

"That was an order," said Lir, and even though she felt helpless, her voice sounded threatening.

"Out of the question, ma'am," said the driver.

"You'll regret that decision," said Lir. She meant that she wouldn't give him the Order of the Blue Sock, as she'd intended. Then she remembered the magic card that she'd made such an effort to hold on to. Maybe she should show it to the driver? She reached into her kimono pocket and, to her surprise, found the unfinished sausage from the night before, now cold and hard. She frowned and, trying to bypass the sausage, rummaged around for the card. As she did so, the outline of something oblong and round appeared through her kimono pocket—something that very much resembled the barrel of a gun. The driver was a perceptive fellow—out of the corner of his eye he noticed the deliberate motions of the Japanese granny and the threatening outline in her silken pocket.

"So, where to?" he asked.

"Entrance fourteen, please. It's the one just after the statue of my grandfather on horseback!" The queen spoke to the driver, channeling the voice of this very grandfather—a war general who resorted to shrieking in moments of danger so that he could be heard across the battlefield (there weren't any megaphones back then). Lir was terrified. And Alice had been poking her for a while now, prompting her to turn around: the bus was being trailed by a police car, its lights flashing and the hotel concierge waving from its window!

"Alright, ma'am. Don't panic, ma'am."

"Faster! As fast as you can!" boomed Lir in the voice of her infamous grandfather, jostling her pocket ever more aggressively as she searched for that darned magic card.

"No need to panic! It's not far!" yelped the anxious driver, seeing the huge gun bouncing in the kimono pocket. "We'll be there soon!"

Meanwhile, the police car had maneuvered out of the flow of traffic and sped up to overtake the bus.

"Even faster! Onward, my dear lad!" ordered the queen.

Upon hearing the police car's siren, Alice squeezed her doll, causing maniacal laughter to drown out all other sounds. The poor driver hunched his shoulders up to his ears—the Japanese girl must be insane, judging by her demented laughter. He was sure they'd shoot him in cold blood, so he did what anyone would do when trying to escape a dangerous situation: he stepped on the gas and urged the bus forward like a charging mammoth. He honked and beeped, and all the other cars turned off the road, while the bus's other passengers grabbed on to their seats and some even got on the floor.

"Bravo darling!" yelled Lir over the doll's crazed laughter, the police sirens, and the honking. The bus drove straight through a red light, crossed the city square, and headed toward the palace's open gates, flanked by gatekeepers in brass helmets adorned with feathers. At the sight of the bus, they began scrambling for their weapons, but when Lir and Alice waved at them through the windshield, they froze in shock.

"Alright dearie, now take a right," Lir directed the driver. He hit the brakes and his mammoth thundered to a stop in front of entrance fourteen. The driver opened the door.

"Alice, darling, did you have fun?" Lir asked her great-granddaughter.

"I certainly did!"

"Let's do it again sometime," whispered Lir, and Alice nodded discreetly.

The pale bus driver watched as the two Japanese women were encircled by people in uniforms, court dress, and liveries; he watched women in dresses with décolletages and long trains spill out of the fourteenth entrance; he watched everyone curtsy and the royal musicians begin playing their horns and drums; he watched the girl being led away by two elderly women and then watched them faint upon hearing the insane laughter issuing forth from her chest, where she clutched a baby doll . . .

"Oh, yes," said Lir, returning to the bus. She'd taken off her black wig, revealing her shaved head with its green mohawk, and the driver's face turned crimson as he grasped his steering wheel. "This dear man deserves the Order of the Lion's Mane for saving the queen and the Order of the Cat's Whiskers for saving the princess. William, write that down!"

NETTLE AND RASPBERRY

ONCE UPON A TIME, TWIN SISTERS WERE born into a family and everyone decided they were two peas in a pod, except their neighbor, a witch, who prophesied that they would grow up to be complete opposites—one would be as horrible as stinging nettle and the other as kind as a raspberry.

"Also," added the neighbor from behind her fence (nobody had asked her, by the way), "the girls will fall in love with the same person. And each girl will be bestowed with the magical ability to fulfill one—and only one—wish. Moreover, these sisters will turn against each other. Mark my words!" After this declaration, the neighbor immediately moved away, and with that her story ends. As for the sisters, they continued to grow and develop into themselves—one was a brunette and the other a blonde, both were darling and kind, and that's enough about them for now.

Let's pick up sixteen years later, when a strange young man moved to the sisters' town. Every night, he rode his bicycle toward the sea and then returned an hour later by the same route. He did this in winter and summer, in rain or shine. The townspeople warned him that swimming during thunderstorms was dangerous—especially swimming as far out as he did, especially in winter, especially at night. But the young man only smiled in response to all the kind advice. (Who knows—maybe he thought this insane activity was good for his health?) The fact is, he made his own decisions, and every evening at five, he'd fly down the hill on his bicycle toward the sea, and at six sharp he'd climb back up the hill. That's the way it went.

Incidentally, his route took him right past the sisters' house, and one fine evening the young man noticed a red flower, bright as a spark, in one of its windows. He even slowed his pace, thinking that he'd like to grow such a flower in his garden. It wouldn't hurt to find out who lives behind those white curtains, he thought. He raised his cap in greeting to the scarlet bloom. And so it continued—day after day, he'd greet the flower with a tip of his cap on his way to the sea, then bid it farewell on his way back home.

Meanwhile, behind the white curtains life was in full swing. It was the home of Nettle and Raspberry, the blonde and brunette, each one beautiful and kind (but the young man didn't know this). The house was always filled with girlfriends and guy friends who all got along happily, and the prediction from that mean neighbor (who'd said she was a witch, anyway? Hearsay!) showed no sign of coming true. The only thing wrong in the sisters' lives was that neither of them was in love. Of course, they loved their parents, their brother, their grandparents, their friends, and each other—but was that enough for two sixteen-year-old girls? To put it bluntly: no, not nearly enough.

And when the young man moved to their town, some imperceptible thing happened. The sisters, each unbeknownst to the other, had begun to glue themselves to their windows at exactly five and then again at six, staying just behind the curtains. At some point, Raspberry put a red flower in her window—she'd found the withered bud in a broken pot by the side of the road. Only later did she casually mention this to her sister, and Nettle didn't give a second thought to Raspberry's flower until it was too late. Of course, the window the young man always doffed his cap to, once at five and again at six, the window with the magnificent red flower the color of ripe raspberries, was Raspberry's window. But we'll leave the dejected Nettle and blissful Raspberry for now.

One windy November evening at half past five, the young man began swimming toward the shore, fighting the rough waves. But the current was pulling him in completely the opposite direction and, to make matters worse, it had suddenly grown as dark as if night had come early, and rain began gushing from the sky. The shore disappeared from his view, hidden behind the heavy curtain of rain. The young man lost all sense of direction and was left to battle the waves in vain as he was dragged farther and farther out to sea.

It seemed all was lost for the poor fellow when suddenly a red spark flashed in the sky as if emitted from a flare gun. The spark didn't rise and fall, though; it shone steadily in one spot. The young man rejoiced—his arms and legs spun like propellers in a desperate, unhinged butterfly stroke as he charged toward the red beacon. When he finally made it back to the shore, at exactly the spot where his now-drenched bicycle stood, he didn't see any kind of light or fire. Under his bicycle wheel, however, was a wet sliver of something, bright red in the gloom. He picked it up—it felt alive to the touch—and put it in the pocket of his raincoat.

On his way home, passing the house with the potted flower, he tipped his wet cap, bidding goodnight to the raspberry-red beauty. This miracle of nature with fanned-out petals, unknown in species and name, shone in the dark window as if under a spotlight. The bloom was missing one red petal, he noticed, like a six-year-old who'd lost her first tooth.

The man pedaled off, sloshing through the deluge, while Nettle and Raspberry, each at her respective window, sighed with relief and wiped away their tears. Then, as if on cue, they turned on their desk lamps—after having spent the last hour sitting in the dark, gazing anxiously through the slit between their curtains—and resumed their homework.

In the morning, they'd be off to school, where the young man was their algebra teacher. He was strict but sympathetic. Nettle and Raspberry were good students, and though they did sometimes get less than perfect grades, it was never in algebra! It's worth noting that as they matured, the twin sisters had begun to exhibit some differences. Nettle was strong-willed and a bit cunning, while Raspberry was quite the opposite—compliant and quiet, always doing as she was told.

Anyway, life continued. The little town by the sea survived another winter, its residents continually surprised that the math teacher rode his bike back and forth in the snow like clockwork—even on cold and windy January nights that began at four in the afternoon—and steadfastly dove into the sea. There was a rumor that the teacher was soon leaving town, that he was training for a race from Africa to America that entailed nighttime biking in stormy conditions and a swim across the ocean! All his documents were allegedly ready, first and foremost his visa. But actually, the teacher, completely unaware of his imminent departure, was preparing his classes, specifically Nettle and Raspberry's algebra class, for final exams.

As we all know, suffering through finals is rewarded with a celebration—in this case, the school's end-of-year ball. Nettle was secretly sewing herself a dress out of sheer white silk (calm down—at three layers thick, nothing would show through). Raspberry wasn't sewing anything; she didn't even know how to sew. She was a quiet girl without many talents and she kept blushing and making mistakes in algebra class (a recent development). But the young teacher made sure to praise her, even for her low scores, the way good teachers praise underachieving students who try hard. He declared that there were no stupid students in his class and then quietly added, "Raspberry, for you and other hardworking students who just need a little extra time with the material, I'm starting a study group." That's when certain boys—the ones who carried Raspberry's school bag for her from home to school to music lessons to tennis and finally back home (never fighting and even taking turns)—suddenly stopped understanding algebra, began failing assignments en masse, and were genuinely thrilled when their teacher shrugged his shoulders and, with a faint smile, invited them to join the study group.

Nettle, however, remained sharp and quick-witted in algebra, leaving her free to spend her evenings sewing, hissing, grumbling, and ripping at threads—all the while dreaming of the moment when the music would swell and she'd ask the young teacher to join her for the Ladies' Choice Tango, dazzling everyone at the ball! In preparation, Nettle had even started attending ballroom dance classes on Sundays, where she caused quite a stir with her natural talent.

Before long, the two girls passed their final exams without much fuss and the night of the ball arrived. Nettle looked like a slender young bride in her flowing white dress. She stood amid a crowd of giddy boys, all aglow. Raspberry sat quietly at a table with her three page boys and watched with twinkling eyes as Nettle and the teacher danced—it turns out the young man was quite the tango dancer himself, and their performance garnered much applause.

It was Raspberry's own fault that she'd ended up sidelined at the ball with a swollen foot: she'd been helping Nettle sew the hem of her dress the previous evening, when at exactly five o'clock she'd dropped everything and bolted to her window as if summoned by an alarm, knocking Nettle to the floor in the process, then tripping over her, and so on. By nightfall, Raspberry's foot had swollen up, but luckily neither Nettle nor her dress were hurt— thank goodness!

"That's what you get for running to the window like a madwoman at five o'clock," Nettle had said with a sinister glint in her eye as she brought her sister a heating pad later that night.

As the ball came to an end in the early morning, Raspberry limped home while everyone else, led by the young teacher, went to the mountains to watch the sunrise. The teacher's head was spinning from the dancing (and from the wine). He thought of sweet Raspberry, quietly watching him from afar, her gaze fixed yet anxious, and his chest swelled with inexplicable joy as he walked ahead of his students along a steep path over a chasm.

At the most dangerous spot, the teacher stopped at the chasm's edge to let each of his students pass; he didn't want anyone to fall. After all, everyone was tired, they'd been drinking, and the girls were wearing heels. He didn't consider that these children had grown up in the mountains and knew them as well as goatherds. Regardless, there he stood when, out of the blue, Nettle began to dance on a rock above the chasm, attracting everyone's attention. Suddenly, the rock teetered. The teacher lunged toward Nettle to catch her. But something went awry: Nettle must have gone in a different direction, or the teacher miscalculated the strength of his leap. Either way, he found himself in the open air above the chasm. His legs were still treading wildly, but it was all in vain—by the looks of it, this would be his final dance, a hopeless dance of death.

The wind whistled and clapped around him; his heart sank, and the dumbfounded students watched his tiny, awkward figure flipping through the air, trying to grab hold of something—anything. A girl began wailing madly. (Undoubtedly, it was Nettle.)

The teacher plummeted down and every hand-hold rushed upward past him, escaping his grasp, when suddenly a bright red spot blinked into view from down below. It flew up and thrust itself into his hand and the teacher clung to the mysterious thing, almost dislocating his shoulder, but he was alive! He dangled there, gripping a root or branch, over what was, at that vantage, a not-so-deep chasm; he could see the sharp tips of jagged rocks about thirty feet down.

He hung on, his legs swinging, feeling hopeless for a long moment. But it wasn't for naught that the teacher biked and swam—his mighty arms didn't fail him. Five minutes later, he was sitting in a tiny notch on the cliff face, hugging the craggy trunk of the tree that had saved his life. Something dangled off a branch that stretched over the chasm, flapping in the wind like a small flag: it was a bright red petal, the remnants of a flower, a sign that this scraggly sapling had been celebrating the coming of spring just moments before.

For some reason, the teacher was compelled to risk his life again—he reached over the chasm, plucked the petal, and stowed it in his pocket. He sat there on almost nothing—the notch was a comma in the stone book of the mountain—clutching the cliff face with his fingernails, his feet pressed against that spindly trunk. He trembled in the sudden wind—a sign that the sun was rising above the mountains, though the teacher remained in gloom.

Climbing up wasn't an option; the mountain formed a so-called "negative angle" above him—meaning it hung over the poor teacher. Mountaineers are familiar with such treacheries and climb negative angles only with the aid of safety ropes and in full gear. Our teacher, wearing his new leather dress shoes, was ill-suited for such an ascent. But climbing down, as mountaineers well know, is even more dangerous than climbing up. On the descent it's hard to see where to put your foot. To make matters worse a cluster of sharp crags lay in wait down below like a frenzy of sharks with mouths agape. The teacher didn't dare move an inch. He grew numb from the cold. Time slowed. At daybreak, the light turned gray around him. He could now see deeper into the chasm, though still not to its very bottom. A dense, ropy fog churned around the crags, shrouding what must have been a brook—it sounded like someone had left the shower on, a cold one at that.

Some sort of endearing, rather large birds (eagles or something of the kind) flew overhead, then perched nearby and—as if anticipating something—began preening their feathers and cawing vociferously. They made the same sound impatient teens make when they're at the movies and it takes too long for the feature to come on.

Three hours later, the whole school had heard that the young math teacher had fallen to his death.

"He was too good for this world," mourned the female teaching staff. At first, everyone said they should call a rescue team and a helicopter, but a helicopter wouldn't fit in the narrow chasm, plus it was too dangerous. A better idea was to call the mountaineers up at base camp, but, as it turned out, there were no telephone lines to reach them up there.

As for Nettle, she hung around school for a bit and then suddenly nodded to herself and ran off without a word. She burst into her house and tiptoed to her room, noticing along the way that the light was on in Raspberry's room. Once her bedroom door was shut behind her, she got under the covers and dialed a phone number. It was the number of a forest firefighter and helicopter pilot who was hopelessly in love with Nettle and had repeatedly invited her on helicopter rides. In fifteen minutes' time, a helicopter landed in the sisters' backyard and a sullen, puffy-faced Nettle climbed into the cabin and asked the delighted firefighter to be taken to Death Chasm. Half an hour after that, having descended as far as possible from the hiking trail, they discovered the fallen teacher—some-how balancing in a seated position atop an almost vertical cliff, clinging to the rock face with his fingernails, his feet pressed up against some kind of root.

He didn't dare wave in greeting, just nodded care-fully as if to say, "Yes, I'm here."

In fact, the gust of air from the helicopter blades almost blew him off the cliff, but the astute firefighter retreated just in time and then threw down the rope lad-der. After thirty more minutes of struggling, tilting, and ups and downs, the helicopter got in position and the rope ladder must've finally dangled over the right spot, since it suddenly grew taught as a line that's hooked a fish. And so it had: the teacher's face, purple from the cold, appeared in the helicopter doorway and he clambered into the cabin.

Upon seeing Nettle, his expression became teach-erly; he was ready to reprimand her for everything he'd thought of over the past hours. But upon seeing him, Nettle burst into tears on the teacher's shoulder with such intense relief (joy, even) that all he could do was retrieve a handkerchief from the pocket of his tattered suit and, after peeling his student off him with difficulty, wipe her eyes and red nose. As he pulled out the handkerchief, a bright red petal fell from his pocket and fluttered to the floor. Nettle was about reach for it when the teacher took hold of her nose and began wiping it with such zeal that the poor girl was temporarily blinded with completely new tears, and the teacher was able to pick up the lost petal and carefully return it to his pocket.

Soon after, the helicopter returned to the sisters' backyard. The teacher shook the hand of the firefighter, who was busy smiling at Nettle and insisting on taking her to a dance club that evening.

"I'll pick you up and drop you off. I've got plenty of kerosene!" Then he mumbled, "You can come too, whatever your name is," continuing to stare at Nettle. But eventually, the firefighter had to whirr away; his night shift was coming to an end, and he flew off smiling while the other two passengers went their separate ways, sullen and exhausted.

As soon as the teacher walked through his door, he placed the red petal in a crystal bowl filled with water. The first petal, the one he'd found that night on the beach, floated there, too, fresh as ever! The teacher stood above the bowl, collecting himself. He needed to recover from the long hours he'd spent on death's doorstep, but instead of taking a hot bath, he felt compelled to examine his new find and try to make sense of what was happening to him. Twice now, he had nearly died, and twice he had not only escaped death but miraculously found a mysterious red petal at the very spot he was saved. Still contemplating this, the teacher finally meandered to the bathroom, where he began to slowly take off his suit, which was torn in three places—both armpits and the seat.

We'll leave him for now, though not before noting that he was a strange man. For instance, the math teacher believed that everything was still ahead of him, and he wasn't yet set on his profession. He hadn't yet decided who he wanted to be. What's more, he sometimes (after certain lessons) thought about becoming a floriculturist. Flowers don't yell, or throw books, or fight. You can talk to flowers, explain things to them, and you can change them, cultivate new varieties—that wasn't possible with students. Yes, he needed to change professions; his job was becoming as deadly as a lion tamer's! After all, he'd just fallen into a chasm because of an overzealous student. But his nightly swims in icy water sure paid off. *Without all that training, I would probably be a smorgasbord for a flock of birds right now*, joked the teacher to himself.

Moreover, he'd already started attempting to cultivate flowers—from one petal. He had read that some petals were capable of taking root, so every morning the teacher looked over his botanical trophy in hopes of finding new growth. The petal had remained fresh and whole, floating in the water without wilting, but it hadn't sprouted any roots. Now there was a second, identical petal. The petals gleamed in the crystal bowl, their crimson light refracted by its sharp edges.

•

Meanwhile, Nettle went straight to her sister's room. The light was on and Raspberry was sitting in an armchair, her head hung low.

"What's wrong?" asked Nettle. "Does your foot hurt?"

Raspberry didn't answer.

"Take some aspirin," said Nettle without any sympathy. She was in a great mood after rescuing the teacher and her sister's woes annoyed her. "Do you want me to bring you some?"

Raspberry remained silent.

"So you know?" asked Nettle. "That it was my fault?"

Raspberry looked at her with sunken eyes.

"But he's alive!" said Nettle. At once, Raspberry turned the exact color of a ripe raspberry and burst into tears. She covered her face with her hands, but the tears streamed through her fingers.

"I rescued him in a helicopter! Andrei, the firefighter, helped me. He's been chasing after me since winter— remember we went to the fire station on a field trip?" Nettle rambled excitedly. "So I called him and we saved the teacher—he was down in Death Chasm. Andrei is really good at flying a helicopter. It was such a narrow spot we almost crashed! The rotor didn't even fit! He promised to teach me how to fly."

Raspberry continued weeping, unable to stop.

"Cut that out!" ordered Nettle. "You done?"

"Done," whispered Raspberry with a shuddering breath.

"And give me a hug!" demanded Nettle. The sisters hugged. Raspberry continued sniffling.

"Listen, Raspberry," said Nettle, stroking her sister's head. "Do you remember that old neighbor of ours? The so-called witch? The one who made that prediction about us . . . remember? Mama told us about her when we were kids."

"I remember," said Raspberry in a small, barely audible voice.

"Remember she said we'd each have a magical power?"

"Yes."

"You've already discovered yours, haven't you?"

"I don't know," said Raspberry.

"What did you do?"

"I didn't do anything," whispered Raspberry. "I just . . . imagined it, that's all."

"What did you imagine? Tell me!" demanded Nettle.

"I can't. I can't say."

"You have to tell me! You have to! Tell me! I need my magic, too!"

Raspberry was speechless. She felt bad, but she couldn't help her sister.

"Fine, don't tell me," said Nettle. "Your wish is the same as mine. Right? I thought so. That was the prediction, Raspberry—that we'd want the same thing. But that doesn't mean your wish is more important than mine. I'll get my wish, too. Remember that. I saved his life and I deserve him! I don't need any magic to get what I want—I can do it on my own! There are plenty of people who can help me—lots of boys like me; they'll do anything for me. But all I care about is that he loves me."

"But you can't make someone love you," said Raspberry.

"Sure you can—he's still young and he doesn't know how lucky he'd be to have me. When we were dancing together, I think he felt it. But then he asked Cranberry to dance. He just hasn't figured out how lucky he is yet! Did you see them? Cranberry is such a horrible dancer!"

"I don't remember."

"Right, you were stuck sitting with your injured foot. What good is your magic if he didn't even ask you to dance? I bet you wasted your magic on something stupid, didn't you? What was it?"

"I don't know . . . I had this dream . . ."

"About what?"

"I don't remember."

"Tell me!" insisted Nettle. "Was it about the sea? The mountains? The forest?"

"I don't know."

"But your dream came true, didn't it? Then you've had enough! It's my turn."

"I don't remember anything," Raspberry repeated quietly.

Nettle thought for a second, then began a new line of attack.

"What are you always brooding about? Tell me! Just tell me! You've never kept any secrets from me! We're the closest two people in the world!"

"I can't."

"Why not? What'll happen?"

"I can't."

"You're so horrible!" yelped Nettle. "The witch predicted right: that I'd turn out to be nice and you'd turn out to be cruel!"

"Enough," said Raspberry, scowling. When they were younger, it always went like this. Nettle could tease her quiet sister for a long time, but when Raspberry was finally pushed over the edge, there was nothing that could be done. She would stay silent for weeks.

"Fine! When I figure out whatever it is—and I will figure it out—I won't take any pity on you. Just watch! The witch's prediction was about both of us, so I'll find my magic too. And I'm going to be ruthless!" cried Nettle hysterically.

Raspberry remained woefully silent, shaking her head. Nettle woefully shook her head back, mocking her sister. The two identically frustrated faces mirrored each other precisely—the noses moving back and forth like pendulums—only one head was blond and the other dark as night.

As for the teacher, he came out of the shower and once again stood before the crystal bowl that held the petals. He thought for a second and then added a grain of sugar and half an aspirin tablet to the water—an elderly biology teacher had taught him to do so. Food for each of the petals, he thought. And only after that did the teacher tend to his wounds.

Meanwhile, Nettle was far from sleeping. She wrote the teacher a letter, inviting him to a birthday party, then signed it: "Cranberry." She dropped the sealed envelope in the mailbox, laughing to herself. She'd typed the letter so the teacher wouldn't be able to recognize her handwriting. Cranberry's party was in two days, and Nettle put all her strength into preparing for it. She hatched a devious plan. Finding her magic could wait—Nettle was intelligent enough to do whatever she had to without the help of magic.

First, she came up with a simple way of taking care of one problem: Raspberry had also been invited to Cranberry's party and was planning on going, despite her injured foot. She'd already picked out a little red ensemble and intended to wear their mom's flats so she wouldn't limp too much. The morning of the party, she was rosy-cheeked and quietly singing to herself when an impatient Nettle barged into her room.

"I know you're mad at me, but you'll be thanking me in a minute. I just ran into our former math teacher. He sends his best and said that, if it's okay with you, he'd like to stop by and see you tonight! Everyone will be at Cranberry's party, but the poor guy wasn't invited. So he wanted to come see you. What do you think?"

"What for?" asked Raspberry, blushing.

"Ah, so now the wicked witch speaks!" yelped Nettle, triumphantly. "What for—I don't know. He must have something to tell you."

Raspberry blushed even harder in response.

"Or he just feels bad for you because of your injured foot. Obviously, he doesn't know you've decided to go to the party."

"No, I'm not going," said Raspberry instantly.

"Oh, you aren't? Then can I borrow your red skirt with the matching top for a night?"

"Go ahead," said Raspberry, frowning. Maybe she was planning on sitting at home and waiting for the teacher in that very outfit . . . that's what Nettle thought, anyway. Smiling triumphantly, she took the clothes out of the wardrobe and walked out. Have fun waiting, Nettle smirked to herself. The door slammed shut and Raspberry began rummaging around her wardrobe in search of something else to wear—a different skirt and blouse—but the door cracked opened again and Nettle's sly face peeked into the room.

"No need to rush! He said he'd come sometime between seven and nine. Actually, can I borrow your little black hat, too? And your black heels? And your red bag?" With those words, Nettle burst into Raspberry's room like a hurricane, upending everything. On top of the things she'd asked for, she grabbed a pair of black tights, some face powder, and a pearl necklace (in effect, all of Raspberry's riches) and left her sister to clean up. Raspberry limped around her room, picking up spilled beads, rings, socks, and even pressed flowers that had fallen out of a notebook, while Nettle rushed into town, likely to a store—she'd left behind a shattered piggy bank and her own room in the same messy state as her sister's. She returned shortly holding a paper bag, locked herself in her room, and grew quiet.

A bit before five, Nettle slipped out her window and ran down the street, ducking so that Raspberry wouldn't see anything. Nettle was wearing the red outfit and black heels, her hair was hidden under the black hat, her cheeks were flushed scarlet as raspberries, and she practiced a limp as she paced back and forth until a familiar bicycle appeared, racing downhill. The cyclist tipped his cap in greeting to the red flower in the window (the curtains fluttered) and then, with surprise, lifted it again as he spotted the young girl limping along the street. The girl demurely nodded, her face blushing.

"Hello there!" the teacher's voice sailed over the street. Then he disappeared, as did Nettle, while Raspberry sat in vain at her window. At six, as always, the teacher zipped past in the opposite direction, raised his cap, and rode off. He didn't come by to see Raspberry at seven, or at eight, or at nine. At nine thirty, though, Nettle came home, all happy and disheveled. She returned the crumpled red clothes and everything else she'd borrowed to the ashen Raspberry, then plopped down in front of the TV with her grandmother and brother.

She told no one what had happened: an hour and a half after seeing the teacher on the street, Nettle arrived at Cranberry's birthday party looking completely unlike herself—golden-haired and rosy-cheeked. Her eyes twinkled, her skin was aglow, and her mouth looked like three raspberries (two at the bottom and one on top). To top it all off, she limped theatrically.

"Raspberry! You're feeling better!" everyone greeted her. "Where's Nettle?"

"Nettle isn't well—poor thing overexerted herself," said the cunning Nettle. "She's the one who saved our math teacher! Didn't you hear? Nettle made Andrei the firefighter fly his helicopter right into Death Chasm! The firefighter is completely in love with Nettle! Our teacher didn't tell you anything? By the way, where is he?"

"Over there!" The kids giggled—the teacher, still wearing his cycling suit, was sitting at a table surrounded by his former students. "He just showed up!"

"I guess he remembered my birthday!" bragged Cranberry.

Nettle smiled venomously.

"You mean, he showed up uninvited?" she said in Raspberry's voice.

The teacher looked curiously at the overly rouged Raspberry. He could barely recognize her: the fair-skinned girl's eyebrows were uncharacteristically black (why she'd colored them was unclear to him) and her movements were unusually jerky. It was as if she'd been replaced. Not to mention, Raspberry immediately ordered a tall glass of champagne and began boisterously laughing and dancing, despite her injured foot.

And then she started yelling: "Attention! I want to tell everyone about the man I love. I love you, my dear math teacher! Even though it was Nettle who saved you, I am the one you should love! Come to my house tonight! I'll open my window for you, the one with the red flower! It has already begun losing petals—soon it'll die and I'll die with it! So hurry, dear teacher!"

Nettle clambered onto the table and, her feet planted amid all the plates, loudly crooned Tchaikovsky's "I love you beyond measure," and launched into a belly dance. All the guests were in absolute shock! Some of their faces were frozen in pitiful smiles, Cranberry burst into tears, and all the boys averted their eyes from the spectacle. The teacher, however, calmly waited until Nettle (Raspberry) finished her aria, then stretched out his hand with the words "May I call you a taxi?"

"Are you trying to get rid of me, my love?" yelped Nettle melodramatically. "Me, Raspberry, who loves you more than life itself? Fine, fine!" And with that Nettle, blushing like a raspberry, feigned sobbing and took off (forgetting all about her limp). And for once, none of the boys ran after her to escort her home. Once outside, Nettle ripped off her blond wig and hid it in her purse, then returned home the normal way—through the front door—after which our cunning actress changed and knocked on Raspberry's door, holding her things. She put the wrinkled, stained suit on Raspberry's bed.

"Did he stop by? That silly teacher?" she asked.

Raspberry was sitting silently; she wore a white blouse and black skirt. She looked pale and sickly and gave no response to her sister.

"Oh, right!" exclaimed Nettle. "He was at Cranberry's party all night! He showed up uninvited, sweaty as a horse in his cycling suit. He danced with Cranberry, if you can believe it. He danced with every-one—though not with me. He was having a really good time, maybe he forgot about you?"

Raspberry's blue eyes were fixed on the wall.

"Fine," Nettle said abruptly. "I admit it: he wasn't planning on visiting you. I ran into him in town and, I confess, I asked him to visit you. I said, 'She's in love with you, maybe you could stop by and see her? She loses sleep over you.' He was like, 'Oh, I don't know, I'm busy . . .' So I told him you're obsessed with him. I kept insisting that he come over. I said, 'If you do it, I'll tell you a secret.' And he agreed! What an idiot!

"So I told him that it was Cranberry's birthday and that we were all going to her party, but that you weren't. I told him you weren't invited, that no one really likes you, you don't have any friends, you aren't ever invited places, and so on. I wanted him to feel bad for you. And I said firmly, 'I'll tell her you'll come after seven.' But then—get this—he said, 'I would come but why do you have that ugly red flower in your window? Why would anyone want such a tacky plant?' He said, 'It shows a lack of taste on Raspberry's part!'"

Finally, Nettle added, "Let's throw that plant away, okay?" and looked inquisitively at her sister. Raspberry continued staring at the wall, but her eyes became glazed and fiery, like those of a child with a high fever.

Suddenly, as if possessed, Raspberry screamed, "No! No! No!"

"Mama!" screamed Nettle. "Mama! Raspberry is sick!"

Their mother came in with a thermometer, and ten minutes later the whole panicked family put Raspberry to bed and called a doctor—Raspberry was running a high fever. The fever hadn't improved by the next evening, when, at five o'clock sharp, the young teacher bravely rode past the sisters' house. He tipped his cap in greeting to the red flower, but the flower looked pretty miserable—somehow its three petals had darkened and lost their luster. And by the time the teacher returned from the sea, he saw that the flower had fallen out of the open window. The pot had cracked, the stem was bent and broken, and the red petals lay on the pavement like dark droplets of blood. The teacher stopped, gathered up the pot, and gingerly put it back in the open window, and as he did, one of the petals fluttered off. The teacher picked it up and thoughtfully put it in his pocket. When he got home, the petal joined the other two in his crystal bowl, and he added another grain of sugar and half an aspirin tablet—a portion of food for the newcomer.

The next day, word spread that Raspberry was gravely ill. Nettle shot through town like a meteor: running to pharmacies, fetching doctors, lugging bags of lemons home from the store, and so on. Twice she saw the teacher—he was tinkering in his garden, tilling a piece of land the size of a dishrag—and both times, she engaged in lengthy discussions with him about her sister's health. And every day at five, Nettle was planted in her window to greet the teacher with a wave. The other window was empty—the teacher never again saw the broken pot with the red flower.

A day later, Nettle and the teacher bumped into each other again. Nettle was returning from the pharmacy hauling an oxygen tank and a bag of cranberries and asked the teacher for help carrying the heavy things home. He agreed and, for the first time, saw the inside of their house. A tense silence hung in the air; it wasn't like a normal home with a TV murmuring, a phone ringing, a grandma offering oatmeal with a side of discipline to her grandson—no, inside this house, it was empty and dead. The only sounds, coming from a barely open door, were heavy breathing and whispering (likely Nettle's parents).

"What happened to the flower in the window?" whispered the teacher, unable to help himself (when they'd come up to the house the flowerpot was nowhere in sight).

"Shh!" hissed Nettle. "Later!"

The teacher immediately left, barely saying goodbye, and Nettle thought to herself, Wow, he noticed!

The flower had its own strange story. Nettle pushed it out the window one evening for no particular reason, she just felt like it. She did it quite impulsively and carelessly, not even trying to muffle the sound of the pot hitting the pavement. She did look over at her sister right afterward, though—had she noticed anything? Would the sickly girl drag herself out of bed in search of the ruined flower, basically her deity? But Raspberry didn't even flinch and remained still. Later, decided Nettle, I'll pick it up and bring it back in. Hopefully she won't notice. But soon after, Raspberry took a turn for the worse and Nettle spent all night at her bedside, changing the cold compress on her sister's head. By morning, Nettle had been replaced by her grandmother, and only later in the day, once she'd awoken from a deep sleep, did Nettle go to Raspberry's room to check her window. She found the flowerpot back on the windowsill, as if nothing had happened. The flower was still alive, even though the pot was cracked, but its stem was fractured, and only two petals remained. Did it jump back up here? Nettle was dumbfounded. Maybe it's magical? She looked at her sister, who was still unconscious in bed, and decided that this overly resilient plant had to go. This time she didn't even try hiding what she did. So the flower ended up in the trash and began its march down the path everything takes to leave this world—a path that leads far, far away into the realm of forgotten things that lies deep in the heart of the earth. Along with the flower, Nettle threw away something else—something that needed to be removed from the house before anyone found it.

Before long, Nettle was sent back to the pharmacy and was stopped by many people along the way—the whole town knew that Raspberry was not well. She spoke to the teacher, too, and on her way back home she made a loop to walk past his place again—but by then it appeared to be locked up. The teacher must've left for his nightly swim a bit ahead of schedule, so Nettle headed home with a heavy heart.

Indeed, the teacher had left. He'd left town on a new

bicycle on a dizzying journey across the mountains and into the surrounding valleys. He was searching for something (after having consulted with the local residents). His last conversation with Nettle had gone like this:

"How's your sister?"

"Oh," Nettle lit up at the sight of the teacher. "She's still in moderately critical condition." Nettle teared up. "I can't bear to look at her. I'm with her all night and then all day I run around to pharmacies and doctors, distracting myself from the horror."

"Last time we spoke, I asked you about that flower . . ." said the teacher, as if in passing. "The thing is, I wanted to ask you for a cutting."

"Oh, dear," said Nettle, shaking her head. "It must've been very windy . . . it was blown off the windowsill . . . I didn't tell poor Raspberry about it, she would've surely died of grief . . . I picked it up, but the pot was cracked . . . I put it back in the window . . . I meant to buy a new flowerpot . . . but I was so busy, I forgot all about it. And the flower wilted completely, so I threw it in the trash. Luckily, Raspberry hasn't noticed it's gone, since she hasn't gotten up . . . Her foot keeps getting worse . . . ever since the ball, but you probably don't remember. She didn't even dance, the poor thing . . ."

"I don't remember."

"I kept telling her to go see a doctor, but she's as stubborn as an ox."

"So she hasn't left the house since then?" asked the teacher cautiously.

"Not since then."

"What do the doctors say?"

"Some say the foot needs to be amputated. Some say it's too late for that, it would only cause her more suffering." With that, Nettle began crying and pressed herself into the teacher's shoulder.

"Too bad about the flower," said the teacher, his tone sharp.

"Yes, too bad. Now it's somewhere at the town dump," said Nettle apologetically. "If I had known, I would've given it to you."

"But I saw her somewhere . . . at some party," muttered the teacher.

"Oh, yes, I completely forgot! Yes! I'm remembering now, Raspberry did go somewhere, all dressed up in red—I'd forgotten. She shouldn't have gone out; she was already feeling unwell. 'I have to tell him,' she was saying, over and over like a crazy person. She only made it worse for herself. I tried talking her out of it, but she said it was more important than life itself. That silly girl, what could be more important than life? Right?"

That had been the end of it.

•

And so, the teacher biked on and on along the mountain road until evening, when he found what he was looking for: the massive town dump that smoked and reeked from half a mile away—no wonder it had been sequestered away from the townspeople. It was getting dark as the teacher rode, his bike bouncing along a bumpy path lined with chaotically colorful piles of refuse. Broken glass and scraps of metal littered the path, so the teacher dismounted and carefully walked his bike. Quite soon, he heard the distant roar of a motor coming from the far end of the dump—he hopped back onto his bike and sped off, plowing ahead blindly, no longer trying to spare his tires. It was clear that, in the distance, the next garbage truck was making its way through the surrounding hills toward the town dump. He could already see it down below, humming like a dung beetle, approaching with a new batch of garbage that would soon pour down and smother the earlier trash—specifically that morning's lot.

The teacher now saw where these dumpster ships docked and set down their loads. It wasn't far from him. But the garbage truck had already arrived; it began lifting its back, and in the advancing darkness, the teacher began quickly chucking aside torn books, broken chairs, and other junk. He was scrambling to find the plant before it was too late and didn't notice that a heap of construction waste hung right over him . . . but then, in the depths of trash, he saw a brief red flicker like a faint signal or spark. The mighty teacher heaved aside a heavy box of broken tiles, then a tattered suitcase, and at last saw his flower. It looked like a broken arrow—a green zigzag lying on crumbles of brick, its final two petals gleaming. Its root disappeared into a plastic trash bag. Carefully freeing the root, the teacher suddenly saw what appeared to be a blond, curly head at the bottom of the bag, and his heart almost stopped in horror. It looked like Raspberry's hair. The teacher picked up the bag and immediately understood: whoever threw away the flower had also disposed of a blond wig.

Just then, a petal fell from the barren flower and drifted off to the side. Still gripping the trash bag, the teacher lunged with the agility of a goalie and caught the petal—and at the same moment, a terrible rumble shook the surrounding hills. An avalanche of rock and brick came crashing down mere inches from the teacher. The dump was shrouded in a cloud of white dust. Then everything went quiet; only a faint echo reverberated through the mountains.

On the very spot where he and his bike had stood only seconds ago towered a veritable mausoleum of rocks. Buried under them was his brand-new bicycle—that miracle of engineering with thirty speeds, puncture-proof tires, and a special uphill function—which he'd only recently bought with the money he'd earned from a year of hard work. He, too, could've been crushed under those rocks, and no one would've ever found his unmarked grave. The teacher put the captured petal in his cap for safekeeping, whispered, "Farewell, bicycle," and ambled back toward town. As for the flower, of course, it had died—now it resembled a shriveled black rag. The teacher carried it, grieving its loss, the rest of the long way home.

When he got there, the teacher took the flower out of the trash bag (still containing the blond wig) and buried its remains in his newly dug garden under the light of the bright southern stars, then watered it generously. The last petal, he lowered gently into his crystal bowl where the others floated, bright red and perky as ever. And the wig belonged back in the trash!

That same dark evening, Nettle unexpectedly visited the teacher at his home.

"So this is how you live," she said excitedly, looking around with bright eyes. She grew pale the moment they fixed upon the crystal bowl with the red petals.

"How beautiful! What is that?" she said. "But . . . oh, no, I don't feel well! I need water . . ."

The teacher went to the kitchen but then heard a crash, shattering glass, and a yelp. Nettle lay on the floor surrounded by shards of the broken bowl. She looked up guiltily at the teacher.

"I felt sick, forgive me," she mumbled. "I'll clean everything . . ." She jumped up, ran past the teacher into the kitchen, quickly found the broom and dustpan, and— before the teacher could gather his wits—swept up the whole mess, including the three red petals, and dumped it in the trash.

"I'll buy you a new bowl tomorrow," said Nettle, hurrying out the door.

After her departure, the teacher emptied the contents of the trash onto a newspaper. The petals weren't there. Neither was the wig. The teacher clenched his fists, but it was too late. Too late.

He spent the next two days locked up in his house. He lay around, trying to read, and didn't even ride his old bike to the sea. When he finally did resume his routine, he was stopped by the elderly biology teacher who told him, among other news, that Raspberry was on her deathbed. Even her sister, Nettle, who'd been running constant errands all over town, had stopped going out.

The teacher took his usual route toward the sea, but when he reached the familiar white house, he stopped short and got off his bike. He walked up to the window, now flowerless, paused to listen, then climbed into the room like a thief. Raspberry lay in bed in total silence, her skin fair as white marble. She was gaunt, her eyes were wide open, and still her face was so magnificent that it made him want to cry or pray. The teacher bowed his head, pressing his forehead to the dying girl's hand. Just then, he heard approaching footsteps. He leapt up and climbed back out the window but stayed just outside it. The curtains blocked his view of the room, but he heard someone carefully enter and close the door behind them. It sounded like they'd collapsed onto their knees. Then came the high-pitched, quivering voice of a young girl.

"Dear Lord, please forgive me! Lord, have mercy on her! Please bring her back to life! I know I have sinned in trying to do magic, but I don't want anything anymore! I won't ever do it again! Lord, take my life instead. I don't need magic, save my sister! She didn't do anything wrong. Take me! Have mercy on me, forgive me! Let this be my wish: she may not want to live but I . . . I WISH HER TO LIVE!"

The teacher listened to this drivel, not understanding a bit of it. Soon, others came into the room, muttering "Come now, come now," and led away the girl who'd been babbling as if delirious. Then, complete silence. The teacher stood outside, his forehead pressed to the wall of the house. Passersby stared at him, but he didn't care. In the room, however, something happened. The smallest sound broke the silence that reigned behind the curtain: an inhale—a heavy, wheezy breath. Then another breath . . . and another . . . The teacher couldn't help himself, he stuck his head through the curtains and looked at Raspberry—her eyes had closed and she was breathing!

The teacher jumped on his bike and sped off, not to the sea but toward his home. He stepped over the low fence that separated his garden from the street and there, in the middle of the tar-black dirt, which he'd watered twice a day in frantic hopelessness, was the bright green glimmer of a newly sprouted shoot. The shoot wasn't big—the size of a needle's point. The teacher shut his eyes, not wanting to jinx it. He didn't let himself rejoice—it could just as well have been a stem of burdock or wormwood. Or even a nettle, god forbid.

The young teacher stood up and suddenly felt very wise: until now, he realized, he hadn't been scared of anything because someone was watching over him (when he'd been pulled out to sea, when he'd fallen in Death Chasm, and when he'd almost been crushed at the dump along with his bike). Now Raspberry was sick, and she was the one who needed watching over. But he was somehow certain that Raspberry would recover, and he saw a new future for himself when she did—in it, he'd have more responsibility, a prospect that made his heart skip a beat.

In this future, he and Raspberry would have four children (twin girls and then two boys, one after the other). They would have a two-story house with plenty of room for their cat to chase their puppy. Their garden would be filled with red flowers, so bright they'd be visible even at night, and these flowers would keep everyone safe—after all, flowers are love brought to life, there's nothing magic about them.

So the teacher changed his clothes, bought some juice and a bouquet of peonies, and set off for his first official visit with his future bride. But before all that, he covered the fledgling sprout with a jelly jar, just to be safe.

TWO SISTERS

ONCE UPON A TIME, TWO SISTERS LIVED together in an apartment. They were very poor. For breakfast, they'd each eat a slice of bread and drink a cup of hot water; for lunch, they'd eat boiled potatoes. Though they were very thin, they were tidy, and their apartment was spotless. They went to the grocery store every day—for them, it was an exciting adventure that lasted many hours. They were also library members and diligently exchanged books once a week. They were always neatly dressed—they'd knitted themselves sweaters, socks, mittens, scarves, and berets using repurposed yarn from old wool garments they found in dumpsters. They were always surprised by how much some people threw away. In short, the two sisters managed to fill their days to the brim despite any lack they may have had.

Occasionally, they'd find other interesting things during their dumpster outings, like bundles of old magazines filled with useful advice, dress patterns, and medical recommendations for common ailments; sometimes a sturdy wooden crate. The sisters loved crates and every time they brought home a new find, they'd spend hours cleaning it and deciding where to put it—under the table, on top of the wardrobe, or on the balcony. They already had a lot of crates and a whole plan to make them into beautiful shelves for the entryway.

But things change, and the older sister, who was eighty-seven years old, fell ill. They called for a doctor, but he never showed up, so the younger sister, who was eighty-five, sat at her bedside and rummaged through a shoebox filled with old medicine left by their grandmother, mother, and children. There were unmarked powders, empty bottles, and ointments in tubes with peeling labels. It was clear the older sister was dying; her breathing was laborious and raspy, and she could no longer speak. The younger sister—her name was Lisa—desperately combed through the powders and ointments hoping to find a cure for old age. The week before, when the doctor had visited, she'd said that Rita, the older sister, was dying of old age—an ailment in and of itself.

Lisa scrounged through the shoebox and wept as Rita's breaths grew more and more infrequent until at last she became still. Lisa wailed in grief and dabbed some random ointment on her sister's parted lips. Then, fearing that the old ointment might be poisonous, she dabbed some on her own lips, intending to die along with her sister if that were the case.

Yet right as the ointment began to melt on Lisa's lips, she fell into a sort of dream. She saw figures dressed in black falling from the ceiling and disappearing into the floor. They fluttered down like snowflakes—there were so many of them. Suddenly the air cleared and Lisa woke up. A stranger lay on Rita's bed—a little girl wearing Rita's nightgown, huge on her small frame. She stared up at Lisa.

"Little girl," said Lisa, "what are you doing here? This isn't funny. Where's my Rita?"

"Little girl," said the girl in a high-pitched, defiant voice, "how'd you get here? Where's Lisa?"

"What little girl?" asked Lisa. "I'm no girl!" She reached out to grab the girl in Rita's nightgown and suddenly saw, protruding from the sleeve of her granny sweater, a pale little arm with pink fingernails. Someone else's arm was sticking out of her sleeve! Lisa was terrified. She jerked back and watched in horror as this strange arm retreated into her sleeve. It was as if Lisa's clothes had emptied—she now noticed how loosely they hung on her frame.

"What've you done to me?" cried Lisa.

"Get out of here at once!" cried the girl on the bed and began kicking Lisa, her feet in Rita's hand-knit wool socks. Grannies often wear socks to bed, and Lisa had put those exact wool socks on the cold feet of the dying Rita that evening. Lisa boiled over with anger. She snatched one of Rita's socks off the petulant girl's foot.

"Hey, that's my sock!" screamed the girl, grabbing the sock from Lisa's hand.

"It's Rita's sock," yelled Lisa. "She knit it herself! She darned it!"

"I knit it!" yelled the girl. "I darned it! Are you crazy? I'm Rita!"

"You're Rita?"

"Yes! But who are you, you rotten girl?"

"I'm Lisa!"

Naturally, this debate escalated into a scuffle and then tears.

"I get it," said Lisa finally. "I'm Lisa and you're Rita. Rita, you didn't die?"

"Of course not," said Rita. "Last night I heard you crying, but I knew I wouldn't die."

"Did you feel it when I put ointment on your lips?"

"I did—and it was the most disgusting thing I'd ever tasted. My mouth burned, the ceiling started falling, and strange figures dressed in black rained down."

"Yes!" Lisa exclaimed. "I put the ointment on my lips, and it was the most disgusting thing I'd ever tasted, too!

"Where's that ointment?" asked Rita. "We've got to save it!"

"There was barely any left."

"If you'd put any more on me, I might've ended up in a swaddle—can you imagine?" said Rita. "Okay, so how old are we?"

"I'm probably twelve," said Lisa.

"I think I'm thirteen and a half," said Rita.

"What about Mama and Papa?" asked Lisa with tears in her eyes. As the youngest, she was the crybaby and the favorite.

"What do you think?" said Rita, the sensible older sister. "You think Mama and Papa are here to spoil you, like always? You know where they are—they've been at the cemetery for thirty-five years."

Lisa began crying over her mama and papa while Rita, the responsible one, began tidying up. She'd had to knot her skirt at the waist to prevent it from falling off. Lisa watched her sister through tears, thinking about how Rita was always the older one—now she'd start bossing her around and annoying her with things like, "wash your hands," "make your bed," "go buy some potatoes," "listen to Mama and Papa . . ." which reminded her that Mama and Papa were gone, and she broke down once more in tears of grief. Rita picked up the box of medicine and began searching for the ointment. Lisa continued to cry. Rita couldn't find the ointment and the frustration drove her to tears. They each sat in their own corner and cried.

"I don't want to live with you—you're annoying!" wailed Lisa.

"You think I want to live with you? I've spent eighty-five years trying to teach you how to be tidy and you still haven't learned! Where'd you put the ointment? You know how valuable it is! We could've been young forever, eternally beautiful, eternally seventeen!"

"Sure, you'd be seventeen, but I'd only be fifteen— and forever at that! No thanks! Everyone's always criticizing fifteen-year-olds, I remember crying a lot when I was that age."

"But life will just pass us by in a flash again," said Rita.

"The ointment is gone, deal with it," said Lisa. "Personally, I want to grow up, get married, have kids."

"Oh, yeah, all that fun again: morning sickness, giving birth, laundry, cleaning, errands, work. The demonstrations and the rallies—god forbid another war! Who wants that? All our loved ones are long gone—I'd like to be where they are."

"And what would I do without you? A sick, lonely granny like myself?" Lisa began sobbing again. She wiped the tears and snot off her stubby nose with her little hand. "Who'd take pity on a poor granny? Who'd bury her?" cried Lisa while Rita resumed the search for the magic ointment.

When it came to be dinnertime, the sisters boiled some potatoes. They reluctantly ate potato and onion soup, then mashed potatoes, then kefir for dessert. What they really wanted was some cake, ice cream, or candy— or at the very least, a piece of bread dipped in sugar.

"How did we eat this slop every day?" asked Lisa, not able to finish her potatoes.

"Not much choice—our pensions are small."

"And why do we have seventeen old crates?"

"We wanted to make shelves for the entryway, remember?"

"Who cares? I hate this apartment! We live in squalor," said Lisa. "And where are all the toys?"

"Remember, your granddaughter took them three years ago."

"Oh, right, last time she visited she threw out all of her old toys—the ones she used to play with when she was young."

"We'd been saving them for her children, and she came and threw them out."

"What about my bike?" asked Lisa.

"Your grandson took it apart. He wanted to use the parts for a car, but he lost some of the screws."

"Right. And he broke our sewing machine. I remember now."

"Darling children," said Rita. "How surprised

they'll be when they see two little girls instead of their grannies!"

"They won't recognize us," said Lisa. "They'll kick us out of the apartment and start investigating who killed their grannies and how some kids started living in their place. Can you imagine?"

"You're right! And what about the mailwoman—will she give us our pensions?"

This made the sisters seriously worried. Their mailwoman would bring Rita's pension in two days and Lisa's in a week. They needed to come up with a plan.

And what if the neighbors saw them? Their neighbors were very active—always listening to music, having loud arguments, and dropping dishes. Their teenage children liked to hang out on the stairs, smoking and using language so foul that the sisters' ears burned and their eyes clouded over as they passed them on the way out of the building. And when they returned home, the stairwell smelled of noxious smoke and the teens continued their loud, unsavory conversations.

Rita and Lisa started thinking up ways to avoid being seen. They could stay out at the park or the library until late, but evenings were a particularly ripe time for teen rowdiness. And in the mornings, the janitor would come—though only when she had free time, and who has any of that these days? The janitor would show up only after the residents had lodged complaints with the newspaper, the town council, even the Supreme Soviet. Even before their magical transformation, the sisters had felt like they lived on the edge of a volcano. The teens kept a close watch on the grannies and from time to time broke into their apartment. It always ended with the grannies in tears, the police showing up, the teens explaining, "We just wanted some water, we didn't steal anything—we don't want your junk," and the filing of an official report. And for a long time afterward, the sisters' coming and going in the stairwell would be accompanied by the teens' loud, hearty laughter.

If Lisa and Rita lived on the first floor, they could've climbed through the window, but they lived on the sixth floor. The only possibility of escape was in the early mornings. By the wee hours, the whole teen gang would usually grow tired and disperse. The sisters knew that they'd all be asleep by 5 a.m. But they'd have to return home at nine, when the coast was clear again—most children were in school, and those who skipped were still either asleep, or—if their unrelenting parents had shoved them out the door to go to school—as far away as possible from both home and school.

The adults of the building were also to be avoided. All neighbors living in the same building typically know each other, whether they want to or not, especially over time—and this apartment building was more than thirty years old. Back when they were relatively young women—fifty-five and fifty-seven—Lisa and Rita had been relocated to a new part of town and given this apartment. Their former building—which was in the center of town—had been bought and first turned into a repair shop, then torn down, and now replaced by a small public square with a sandbox.

Lisa and Rita were happy with the move at first—the building had an elevator and their apartment had a balcony. But for the next thirty years, the sisters were constantly pestered by people looking for a way to relocate them, this time to a much worse apartment or even a different city. These people relentlessly checked in on the sisters, especially once they caught wind of Rita's failing health. They'd offered money, and lots of it, but the sisters were used to their simple, one-bedroom apartment, whose windows faced a small park, and their balcony, where they could get some fresh air when they were trapped in their apartment because of the teens. It was one of these times that the sisters came up with the basket idea. Whoever was home would use a rope to lower a basket from the balcony, and whoever was down below would put her purchases in it for the other to hoist up. This was to prevent the teens from robbing them on the way to the elevator, in the elevator, or on their way out of the elevator. Taking the stairs was certainly not an option—not that they'd had the strength for it in a decade anyway.

But back to the present: the sisters' next hurdle was clothing. It was inconceivable that the girls would wear granny clothes—those carefully patched skirts, still so worn out that they could be used as sieves. The grannies had gotten into the habit of wearing multiple skirts at once, one on top of the other, for warmth as well as for opacity. They'd also worn hand-knit wool cardigans, and Rita had even constructed a winter coat: the front was knit, the back was quilted, the collar was knit, the sleeves were sewn fabric, and the cuffs were, again, knit. She and Lisa shared the coat and considered it to be the latest in fashion. They saw the envious looks other grannies gave them in lines and on park benches. The sisters took turns wearing the coat for special occasions. Children would choke with laughter at the sight of them—absolutely squealing with glee. Yes, life hadn't been easy for the two grannies, but it was nothing compared to what awaited them as little girls.

Rita and Lisa talked all night and into the next day and even ran the kitchen faucet to drown out their conversation. The first time the sisters were children, they would argue, play, and gossip; Rita would discipline Lisa, and Lisa would put up a fight—but they'd been surrounded by adults who set curfews and made sure they didn't speak to strangers or bring home bad grades. Times were hungry. Times were tough. Their mama and papa always stuck together because there were times when fate had separated them. Their parents had entered an unspoken accord, ardently clinging to each other, seemingly always in silent conversation, pausing it only when they spoke to the girls. They even died one day apart, as if they'd planned it. They'd wanted to die together, but it hadn't worked out that way. Mama died a day after Papa; she lay in bed all day and never woke up. At the funeral, people said they were lucky, that it happened only in fairy tales—a couple living a happy life then dying on the same day. But truth be told, these two supposedly happy people didn't die at the same moment. One of them had seen death and understood that they were left alone. One of them had cried.

The day of their transformation, the girls reassured each other that everything was fine: they were young, they were smart, and they could look after themselves. They would toughen up, start exercising, and learn self-defense. Rita would sew clothes and earn a living—after all, she used to sew. They planned on scouring the dumpsters for an old sewing machine. Lisa would learn how to cultivate flowers on the balcony—there was plenty of free soil around, the crates would come in handy, and she could collect seeds at the park. All they had to do was get strong enough to climb up a rope, which would take care of the neighbor problem. The two energetic girls made lots of plans. Though at one point they got in a disagreement, then an argument, then a scuffle—but kids will be kids, and in the end they made up. And finally, they devised a plan for getting their pension from the mailwoman—Rita would get in bed under a mound of blankets and wrap a scarf around her head and face until she was unrecognizable, then sign for it wearing a glove. Lisa would pretend to be her helper from the local school. Then when Lisa's pension was due to arrive, they'd switch roles.

"We can figure everything out," said Rita. "We can get used to anything."

"It's a good thing our grandchildren never visit and our own children are too elderly to come around," added Lisa. "And we don't have a phone!" With that, the girls finally climbed up into their beds and fell asleep.

The next morning was sunny and brisk. The sisters heard noisy children getting ready for school under their windows. For breakfast, they each had one slice of bread and a cup of hot water with dried chamomile. Then the girls began thinking about what to wear on such a sunny day. They couldn't very well wear three skirts and wool cardigans! Rita found some bedsheets (still intact and durable), then got out a stack of old magazines in hopes of learning what children wore these days.

"I'll never wear that," said Rita after looking through the magazine, while Lisa ogled the pages and imagined herself in a white lacy skirt and blouse. Lisa got the old suitcases out of the closet and emptied their contents, her eyes sparkling and her heart racing. She rummaged around for a long time until Rita came out into the hall and saw the mess on the floor.

"We can use these," said Lisa, handing Rita a bundle of ribbons and snippets of lace. In response, Rita reprimanded her and began picking up the fabric scraps and baby things no one needed anymore—rompers, swaddles, beanies the size of oranges, and tiny shirts with mitten cuffs—everything left from grandchildren and great-grandchildren and saved for great-great-grandchildren. Of course, Rita and Lisa bickered all the while, but then they sewed late into the evening. Lisa sewed herself a lacy blouse and Rita sewed herself a modest dress from the bedsheet, trimmed with ribbon from a baby beanie— once blue, the ribbon had long ago faded to gray, but gray and white were an elegant combination.

In short, the sisters were dressed by nightfall. Now came the question of shoes. Luckily, the elderly Lisa and Rita never threw anything away: they had felt boots and galoshes and sandals, though it'd all been lying around for years and was creased and rumpled. They found Rita a pair of sporty shoes—a bit worn out and on trend about fifty years ago—and for Lisa a pair of brand-new sandals so compressed that they were as flat as pancakes. With great effort, Lisa pulled the sandals onto her tiny feet, awestruck yet again by the now-delicate toenails on her pristinely white toes.

"How wonderful youth is," sighed Rita, looking at herself in the mirror—they had a single chipped mirror, a birthday gift from their middle-aged granddaughter.

The girls couldn't wait until morning. When it finally came, they ate their slices of bread, drank their hot water with a bit of last year's mint, and briskly walked out of their apartment. It was May. All the other children were sleeping, skipping school, or falling asleep in school. Then there was the issue of transportation. Before, they were never asked for tickets, since the metro was free for senior citizens (the ticket collectors would zip past them as if they were radioactive). But now the sisters had to walk to the library to exchange their books. They sat in the garden square across from the library, all dressed in white among the pigeons and gardeners, waiting for it to open. Even then, they didn't go in right away. Rita figured that they ought to be in school, so if they went inside in the morning (as they did when they were grannies) the librarian would ask why they were cutting class.

So the girls sat in the garden square, which slowly filled with young mothers with their children and grandmothers with their grandchildren. The mothers sat on benches, socializing, at times screaming out wildly, "Stop that!" or, "Galina, get up!" Most grandmothers stayed close to their grandchildren, hovering like wardens over detainees, but some formed a small line by the swings. The line was well-defined and had strict rules of order, and even if their charges crawled away to the sandbox, entertaining other plans, the grandmothers would forcefully plant the children in the swings when it came to be their turn, whether they liked it or not.

"Ridiculous," noted Lisa. Rita didn't answer. At the moment, life seemed impossibly difficult to her. How would they get through summer vacation? And after that? They were children now—eventually, people would notice if they didn't go to school. But going to school meant being in plain view. And they didn't need to go to school. Not again. She and Lisa were well-read old women, and ever since childhood, the sisters had found chemistry, physics, and especially math to be a bore.

By the time the girls went into the library, it was midday and their stomachs were growling from hunger. The librarian took back the books they'd brought and even allowed the girls to check out new ones—ostensibly for the sick grannies in their care. The plan had worked! But instead of the usual Dickens and Balzac, they checked out Hauff's fairy tales for Lisa and an Italian novel called

Lovers for Rita. On their way home, Lisa wheedled Rita into buying some cheap ice cream, then they absentmindedly turned into the park, where they gobbled up the ice cream while gazing at the boats on the pond.

"Boats," said Lisa.

"My pension comes the day after tomorrow," responded Rita. The sisters continued staring at the pond, sighing and remembering the taste of the hastily eaten ice cream, as evening steadily approached. Rita came to her senses first.

"It's almost six—we've got to get home. At seven, they all skitter outside," she warned, imaging the swarm of teens. The sisters sprinted home, arriving just in time. Only the youngest kids were out in the yard, playing after preschool and daycare—running, yelling, crying—while their parents sat glued to the benches with overflowing bags at their feet. It was the teens' turn to come out just as Rita and Lisa ran inside their apartment and locked, deadbolted, and chained the door.

Rita had big plans for the evening—to knit a new doormat out of fabric scraps. But Lisa begged Rita to use the scraps to sew her a skirt instead. Rita won the resulting squabble. Dinner was kefir. As they drank it, Lisa wailed and Rita clutched an old pillowcase containing the fabric scraps.

"I have nothing to wear!" Lisa sobbed. "I don't even

have a watch! Or a bike! Look at the kids outside; they've all got watches and bikes! And all the other girls have friends, but all I have is you! What kind of childhood is that?!"

"Some childhood, at eighty-five," said Rita.

Lisa choked on her kefir and grew silent.

"You've had a wonderful adulthood," said Rita. "Stop complaining."

"Wonderful? I grew old marching to the beat of your drum," cried Lisa. "I'm going to run away! I don't want to grow old as your underling again!"

"If you run away, you'll end up in an orphanage. Do you know what that's like for a girl your age?"

"At least there are other kids there. And food. And school. Yes, that's where I belong!"

"Didn't you read that magazine article about the orphanage?"

"Yes, all the orphans are waiting for their parents to come back for them. But I've got no one to wait for," cried Lisa. "Mama, Papa, where are you?" And she began sobbing with renewed vigor.

Rita couldn't bear it any longer and handed her the pillowcase, but Lisa kept crying.

"Take your scraps!" yelled Rita. "And quit crying!"

"What about my skirt? Aren't you going to sew me a skirt? I need a skirt!"

"If you go brush your teeth and get in bed, then tomorrow I'll sew you a skirt."

Naturally, Lisa replied, "If you start sewing my skirt now, I'll go brush my teeth and get in bed."

Rita clutched her head and tried to remember what Mama would do in such cases. Remembering, she got up without saying a word and went to the bathroom to take a long shower and collect herself. Unsurprisingly, when she came out, Lisa was laying the fabric scraps out on the floor.

"Tomorrow," said Rita, her voice calm. "Now help me pick these up, and don't forget which pieces go together."

They left early the next morning and returned to the park. It was quite empty—just a few gardeners and some delivery men unloading bottles from a truck as a portly snack bar vendor kept watch. Rowboats and black swans floated on the surface of the pond. The swans plunged their heads into their feathers and groped under their wings like a hand scratching at an armpit. An early-to-rise mother stood yawning at the pond with her toddler. The boy, probably two and a half years old, called, "Swigeons, swigeons!" But neither swans nor pigeons came up to him, understanding that he didn't really mean business.

Lisa and Rita sat down, as they always did, on their favorite bench and fell into a mournful silence. When they were grannies, they'd often come to this bench in the late afternoons. They even had one sort-of friend, though they hadn't caught her full name, only her patronymic: Genrikhovna. And there were two other women they didn't like—the sisters secretly called them Plague and Cholera. They were very different from each other, but both used to work in management. They wore their hair short like emperor Nero, and they both looked like him, too. Though Plague's skirt was a bit shorter.

Genrikhovna, a gentle, intelligent woman, was a retired pediatrician and had no living family, though the sisters didn't know why—she'd never shared that. Plague and Cholera were constantly involved in civil disputes—Plague with her neighbors and Cholera with her family—and because of their volatile home environments, they spent almost twenty-four hours a day outside, sitting on the park bench, eating bread, and feeding the birds. Rita and Lisa were polite old women and felt compelled to listen to Plague and Cholera's daily rants. What choice did they have—this was the only park in the neighborhood, and all the benches belonged to established groups: the old women sat on their benches, while the old men took up at the other end of the park, indulging in games of chance, crowding around people playing dominoes and occasionally chess. When old men happened to walk through the circle of benches occupied by the old women, they were met with a marked silence from some benches and chattering and giggling from others. The silent benches hated men of any age, every last one of them, and this sentiment wasn't new. The vocal benches were occupied by turncoats still hoping to get married.

And so Rita and Lisa sat on their bench as usual. At this early hour, Plague and Cholera weren't there yet, so Rita and Lisa remained silent. They needed to go to the store (where there was always a line), then search through dumpsters for a sewing machine, then run home to sew Lisa a skirt. But they just sat there, rooted to the spot. Soon, an old woman sat down beside them. They froze. It was Genrikhovna. She looked at the sisters with kind eyes.

"Hello, children!" she said. Rita and Lisa looked at each other, then nodded silently. Their manners evaporated and they began acting like real adolescents—they didn't say hello and even bristled at the old woman, who wouldn't leave them alone.

"Girls," said Genrikhovna. "May I ask you something?"

"What?" asked Rita curtly, while Lisa got up with the words, "Let's get outta here." Genrikhovna smiled sadly and closed her eyes.

"You sick?" said Rita, but Genrikhovna didn't open

her eyes. "Lisa, I'm going to run to the pharmacy. You stay here."

"As if," said Lisa. "Corpses scare me!"

"She's breathing, dummy," said Rita. "Feel her pulse."

"No way!" said Lisa. "I told you, they scare me." They spoke just like the kids in the stairwell but omitted the swear words. Rita felt Genrikhovna's pulse.

"We need that stuff for heart attacks—what's it called? Nitro . . . something . . . glycerin. That's it."

"I have some in my . . ." began Lisa but then bit her tongue. Gone were the days when she walked around with a big patchwork bag full of helpful things like nitroglycerin. She hoped Genrikhovna hadn't heard anything, and instead she said, "She's about to kick the bucket, let's go."

"Keep your butt glued to this bench!" ordered Rita. "I'm going to the pharmacy, I've still got some cash left."

Lisa was left sitting with Genrikhovna, who was barely breathing.

"Dumb granny, why didn't you go to the doctor?" she said, then began rifling through Genrikhovna's bag. Surely she'd have her favorite medicine in there, as all sensible old women did. Lisa found some sort of pill and put it in Genrikhovna's mouth. The woman began chewing instinctively, like a newborn, then swallowed. A few minutes later, Genrikhovna opened her eyes. Lisa scooted away from her.

"What's going on? Where am I?" asked Genrikhovna.

Lisa stayed silent.

"Little girl, did you give me some of my medicine?" asked Genrikhovna.

"So what if I did? You looked like a corpse. I didn't take anything from your bag—you can check."

"You saved my life. Could you please walk me home?"

"No. I'm waiting for my sister."

Genrikhovna nodded and stayed seated on the bench. Finally, Rita came running.

"I am shocked by the incompetence of the pharmaceutical personnel," said Rita, then caught herself and continued, "Dumb workers! You need a prescription and they don't sell to kids, anyway . . . told me to call an ambulance but wouldn't let me use their phone! Told me to use a pay phone, but the dang thing was broken."

"Girls, I can't make it home by myself," said Genrikhovna. "My name is Maya Genrikhovna. Please help me; I'll give you a little gift as a thank-you. I have a brand-new silk blouse—maybe you'd like that?"

"Mkay," said Lisa, agreeing to help, and the sisters led Maya to her apartment. Maya didn't suspect for a moment that they were anything but normal little girls.

They brewed her some tea and ran to the bakery to get her a loaf of bread. In return, they received a beautiful, frilly blouse. But best of all, they noticed that she had an old sewing machine. Maya promised to give them more gifts and said she'd call their parents to explain where they'd gotten the blouse.

"We don't have a phone," said Rita.

"Or parents," blurted out Lisa.

"They won't care," Rita insisted.

The sisters made it home right before the kids emerged for their evening outings. Their mothers had returned from work, tired and wound up from the long commute home and the grocery shopping along the way. To escape their wrath and avoid questions about homework and grades, the kids would run outside.

In the sisters' apartment, yet another evening was spent sewing a skirt. Dinner was bread and hot water with mint.

"I don't know how we lived like this for so long," mumbled Lisa, hand-sewing fabric scraps together at three in the morning. Rita was already dead asleep. By morning, Lisa was crying.

"This isn't even a skirt—it's a quilt!" She blubbered, "I'm not wearing it. You can have it."

Rita hated seeing her sister upset, so she sewed two rows of ribbons to the skirt's hem and lined it with an old sheet.

"There, now try it," said Rita. Lisa, still sobbing, put on the skirt and looked in the mirror. Then, sniffling, she put on Maya's blouse and began twirling from side to side, admiring her reflection. But soon she collapsed on the bed, buried her face in a pillow, and said she couldn't stand to wear those sandals anymore. They were awful. A joke. After that, they both fell asleep until evening.

In the cupboard, they had some bread, four potatoes, an onion, and a single beet. Rita woke up from her nap first and, taking pity on Lisa, made borscht and toasted some bread into croutons. Out in the stairwell, boisterous laughter and the clinking of glasses rang out until midnight. And at seven the next morning, when Rita cautiously opened the door to take out the trash, she was startled by an awful racket—two empty bottles had been tied to her doorknob and they rattled loudly as they hit the wall. This was very common, just a hello from the partying teens. Rita cut off three more bottles tied to other apartment doors and found four more in the elevator. Some were soft-drink bottles and two were vodka bottles. Rita gathered them up and brought them home. She could deposit them for a refund. It wasn't much money, but enough to live another day.

Actually, it was pension day. Rita got in bed and Lisa wound scarves around her head and neck. Rita put a glove on one hand and a mitten on the other (the sisters owned only a single glove). When the mailwoman rang the doorbell, Lisa opened the door with a mournful expression, explaining that her great-grandmother wasn't well, a bad case of eczema, and her hands and face were in great pain. But she'd still sign for her pension. The mailwoman handed Lisa the form, Rita signed it in her room, the mailwoman counted out the money, then shouted from the doorway, "Feel better soon!" and, not at all surprised by what had transpired, departed.

But only undemanding grannies could survive on such a small amount of money. They weren't growing—not up, not out, not their feet, only the occasional upper-lip hair and toenail (and they needed only a single pair of scissors to deal with those). For clothes, they could just go on wearing whatever rags they'd accumulated over their long lives.

Rita ruminated anxiously: what were they to do? She knew a few stores set out boxes of rotting fruit and vegetables that grannies would pick through, taking produce for their kompot drinks and soups that they couldn't afford in unspoiled form. And grannies could go to the market, where the rich, lazy vendors thought well of themselves when they offered free samples to destitute old ladies who hobbled along the stalls, weak from hunger, trying the plums, sauerkraut, or farmer cheese. Though, more often than not, the grannies would be shooed away from the merchandise like flies with yells of, "Off you go!" And a child would never be forgiven for such behavior. Children didn't have the right to beg, to sample sauerkraut, or to sell knit mittens on one of the market's side streets. A child like that would be kicked out, or worse, taken to the police.

Rita was a little girl with lots of life experience. She herself had grown up, and so had her children and grand-children—she understood there would be many expenses. But Lisa acted as if she had never been a mother or grand-mother. She'd forgotten all about that and saw herself only as she appeared in the mirror, a beautiful young girl who deserved to be spoiled. Lisa had been like this her whole life—her husband had spoiled her, treating her like a child, and then her children grew up spoiled, too. Now they spoiled their own children and there was no one left to spoil poor, old Lisa.

The next day, it took forever to wake Lisa up, so they had to eat breakfast quickly to get out of the house on schedule. Rita didn't share her troubling thoughts with her sister. She preferred to behave as their deceased mother had—she never complained or asked anyone for help, but she demanded perfect behavior from her children. Also,

Rita planned on buying two toothbrushes and some tooth powder, neither of which the grannies owned, because of their lack of real teeth. She was going to make sure Lisa brushed her teeth twice a day!

Just after breakfast, the doorbell rang. Lisa ran to open it. And before Rita could say anything, a stout, ginger man walked into their apartment.

"It's me again," he said. "Where are the grannies?"

"They aren't home," said Rita, terrified.

"Hm, I was hoping to catch them at this early hour. Mind if I wait for them?"

"They won't be home today."

"Hm. Where are they?"

"They're in the country."

"And what are you doing here?"

"We were just about to leave," said Rita.

"Hm. Why aren't you at school?"

"Scarlet fever epidemic," lied Rita. "We're quarantined."

"Hm," said the man. "Right." He walked around the apartment examining the ceilings, pipes, and faucets, running his fingers along the peeling window frames. "Hm. We'll need to renovate." He went out on the balcony and seemed pleased with the view. "What's with all the crates? Hm. The metro is close by. Good. But there's no phone, if I remember correctly?"

"No." The girls watched him in irritation.

"Mister, we're leaving," said Rita finally.

"Go ahead."

"What about you?"

"I'll stay. I've had scarlet fever—I'm not worried. I'll wait up for your grannies. I have something urgent to discuss with them."

"They'll be in the country all summer," said Rita.

"They won't be coming back!" Lisa squeaked thoughtlessly.

"That's okay. I'll stay. I have time."

"What do you want?"

"I want them to register me as their caretaker."

"Why?" asked Lisa.

"Because that way the apartment won't go to waste."

"What do you mean—go to waste?" asked Rita.

"You know what I mean. One's already at death's doorstep—the mailwoman told me. The other one is on her last legs, too."

"Last legs? Nonsense!" yelped Lisa. "What are you babbling about, young man? And what does it have to do with you, anyway?"

"I was here first."

"What?!" said Rita, her cheeks burning.

"And who are you to talk?" said the man. "You aren't registered in this apartment. It isn't yours."

"Our grannies will never register you! They're going to register us, their granddaughters, err . . . great-granddaughters!"

"You're underage, that's illegal," said the man.

"Leave. Leave now," said Rita.

"No," the man said and then lay down—right on Lisa's bed. He kicked off his shoes, turned to face the wall, and fell into a deep sleep, as if he hadn't slept for a very long time. The sisters hurried to the other room.

"He's crazy. And a crook!" said Lisa.

"Lisa, how many times have I told you not to open the door? Mama told you, and I told you. This is all your fault!"

"But I'm just a kid!" Lisa said and burst into tears. They heard snoring in the other room.

"I have an idea," said Lisa, sniffling. "Let's find that ointment and put some on his lips."

"And then what? Deal with a little rascal instead of a big one?"

"We'll put on a lot."

"They're like that at every age—don't you remember our five-year-old neighbor who used to kick us?"

"We'll take him to preschool and never come back for him."

"I'd feel sorry for him," said Rita.

"Sorry for him? He's trying to kick us out of our apartment."

"No, we can't do that," said Rita.

"Should we kill him?"

"We couldn't manage it."

"We could slit his throat."

"Lisa, you're an idiot."

"I'll kill him!" yelped Lisa.

"That's murder!"

"He's a bully."

"Yes, a bully. But he's got nowhere to live. Nowhere to sleep. Can't you see that?"

"You always have sympathy for everyone but me," said Lisa. "Don't you get it—if we leave, he won't let us back in. He'll change the locks. And if we manage to get him out, he'll break down the door as soon as we're out of the house."

"Okay, how about I dress up like a granny and you act like you called me," said Rita.

"How?"

"Watch."

Rita began frantically dressing in all her old granny clothes. She mixed flour and water and spread the paste on her face, where it dried in lines and folds that she outlined with pencil to look like wrinkles. She put on the glove and mitten and then her glasses. She grabbed her cane, and she and Lisa went to the entryway. They opened the door and slammed it shut.

"Grandma," said Lisa audibly, "we called you because some man wants to live in your apartment!"

"Nonsense!" yelled Rita in a deep, raspy voice and began waving her cane. "Where is he?" Lisa led her to the man lying in bed, his jacket unbuttoned.

"Granny," he said hoarsely, clearing his throat from sleep.

Rita briskly whacked him over the head with her cane.

"Police! Police! Suspicious criminal character!" she yelped. The man grabbed hold of his head and sat up. Rita rapped him once more.

"Lisa, go open the door so the neighbors will hear me and call the police." Lisa ran like the wind to open the door. The baffled man scrambled off the bed, still yawning, grabbed his shoes, and ran past Lisa into the stairwell in his socks.

"Sorry!" he called out and disappeared down the stairs. Lisa triumphantly slammed the door and the sisters ran to hug each other.

"We need a mother," said Rita.

"Or a grandmother," agreed Lisa.

"Maya!" they said in unison.

The sisters quickly got ready and headed out. They had decided to invite Maya to live with them. It would be perfect—especially since she had a sewing machine. They knocked on her door but there was no answer. They stood there for a long time, hammering at the door with their fists and heels until a very angry woman came up from the floor below.

"What's with the pounding, you brats?"

"Sincerest apologies," said Rita. "We've come to visit Maya, but something must've happened—she won't answer."

"Banging like a psycho won't help!" said the downstairs neighbor, visibly relieved. She rang the doorbell of the apartment next door. The door opened a crack and a big, wrinkly ear appeared in the space allowed by the chain.

"Uncle Senya," said the neighbor. "What's with number ten?"

"What?"

"She's not opening up. Should we call the police?"

"Don't know," said Uncle Senya, loudly unlatching the chain and opening his door all the way. Now they saw him in all his glory, wearing a blue undershirt, blue drawers, and an ushanka hat with its ear flaps sticking up and the ties dangling around his face. It looked like he'd shaved as recently as a few weeks ago.

"What's with you?" asked the neighbor.

"I'm sick," said Uncle Senya.

"It's tough to live alone . . ." said the neighbor, nodding at Maya's door. "Just like that and . . . done."

"But if you live with someone, they'll send you to a nursing home," said Senya.

"Well, I'm off," said the neighbor. "My baby is asleep and these two were hammering . . . who are you girls anyway?"

"Maya's family," quickly lied Lisa.

"But not immediate family," corrected Rita.

A fat old woman appeared behind Uncle Senya, barefoot and holding a rag.

"What's going on?"

"Number ten won't open up . . . it's been days . . ."

"We saw her yesterday," Lisa lied again. "And everything was fine."

"Then she must've run out to the store," Uncle Senya said, yawning, then shut his door and drew the chain.

The girls decided to wait outside on a bench. They were scared to go home: what if the ginger man was sitting on the stairs waiting to beat them up? Before long it was evening—it wasn't yet dark, but lights began to flicker on in windows. Toddlers ran around shrieking, intoxicated with freedom, their preschool workday complete. There was music in the air. Neighbors and commuters walked past the sisters—but not Maya. Maybe she felt ill again, and someone called an ambulance? The girls sat outside for a long time—until midnight—then shuffled home.

Miraculously, the stairwell was empty. The girls quickly unlocked their door and ran inside.

"Thank goodness!" they both exclaimed in disbelief. They took showers, ate some leftover borscht with bread, and drank some hot water. "Home sweet home!"

That night, Lisa cried in her sleep. Rita didn't sleep at all; she was worried about Maya. Her soul ached for this near stranger, this old woman about whom they knew so little. She remembered Maya's courtesy, calmness, and tact, even when faced with Plague and Cholera. They constantly sought her advice about their ailments, even though Maya had been a pediatrician—more accurately, a neonatologist—specializing in newborns under a month old. Thus most of the time she just empathized and didn't write them any prescriptions. The elderly Lisa would always butt in, giving detailed recommendations—Lisa loved treating ailments. Come to think of it, Lisa saved my life, thought Rita. She got up from her bed and blew gently on Lisa's forehead, the way their mother used to. Lisa sighed and stopped whimpering.

The next morning, the sisters were back at Maya's door. They rang the doorbell. A long time passed and then, from the depths of the apartment, they heard something move. Half an hour passed. Finally, Maya opened the door; she was sitting on the floor.

"Hello!" exclaimed the girls. "We stopped by yesterday, where were you?"

Maya slowly looked up from the floor, leaning on her arm.

"Were you unwell? We knew it! Do you remember us? We're the girls from the park. You invited us over for tea."

Maya nodded.

"We were worried about you, so we came by. How are you feeling?"

Maya opened her mouth but didn't say anything.

"You can't speak?"

Maya began to cry. She sat on the floor and sobbed.

"You need a doctor," said Rita. The sisters dragged Maya into the bedroom. There was an overturned chair and a broken glass in a puddle of water.

"She must've been bedridden yesterday," said Rita. "Lisa, run home and try to find that ointment!"

Lisa nodded and ran off. Rita did the best she could getting Maya into her bed. She gave her a drink of water, cooked her some porridge, and spoon-fed her. Evening came, but Lisa still hadn't returned. Rita began to worry: where could a twelve-year-old girl have possibly disappeared to? Finally, when it was almost nightfall, Lisa showed up, looking pale.

"I couldn't find the ointment. I looked everywhere

for it. When I left, the teens were already out on the stairs, but I made it to the elevator before they noticed me."

Lisa and Rita decided to move in with Maya. They went back to their apartment only once, to sign for Lisa's pension. They performed the same masquerade for the mailwoman as last time. And this time Rita sternly warned her not to give out their address to anyone. They fed Granny Maya. Rita massaged her, as she'd once massaged her father. They bought her medicine. They called a nurse, who came and administered shots. Maya understood everything and put in great effort to recover, slowly moving her fingers at first, then her hands. After a month and a half she said, "Eh, ooh . . ."

"Thank you," translated Rita.

"Oh, ooh, ugh." (You're good girls.)

By August, Maya Genrikhovna was taking walks in the yard, telling everyone, "My darling granddaughters are visiting."

In September, the girls started school. Maya had arranged everything. The girls went to school happily at first, then (like all kids) reluctantly, and sometimes even put up a fuss in the mornings, especially Lisa. Then again, when they all chatted together in the evenings, Maya was always amazed by how wise and understanding the two little girls were, and before bed she would make the sign of the cross over them and say, "These aren't ordinary children." And the two adolescent grannies slept, both hoping that one day they'd find the magic ointment so they could share it with their dear Maya. Rita dreamed of Maya with their mother's features—young, beautiful, and strict—while silly Lisa dreamed that Maya was a swaddled, crying newborn, and that she and Rita had run out of milk.

And on Saturdays, the three of them sold knit socks and mittens by the metro. Perhaps you've seen them there?

THE STORY OF AN ARTIST

THERE ONCE LIVED AN ARTIST WHO WAS so poor that he couldn't afford pencils or paper, let alone paint or brushes. Sure, he tried to draw on sidewalks with bits of brick, but the street cleaners and police didn't appreciate such art. Our poor fellow would've drawn on walls or fences, but every wall and fence belonged to someone. And that sort of thing had to be done at night, when people weren't ambling about and getting in his way—but who'd want to draw in the dark? Anyway, brick doesn't draw on walls—it just scratches them.

At least the artist had a roof over his head, though his squat could hardly be called a home. In one apartment building, a street cleaner had walled off a small corner under the stairs so he wouldn't have to drag home his brooms, shovels, crowbars, felt boots, and work coat. The street cleaner fashioned a door, complete with a rusted lock, and hung up a notice advertising an affordable room for rent (no A/C). This is where our artist slept, on the floor atop his overcoat, happy at least not to be sleeping

169

outside where it was cold, rainy, and anyone could rob him of said overcoat.

How the artist ended up so penniless is a long story— suffice it to say, he was swindled the same way so many unsuspecting, penniless people are. They're promised big payouts for their modest apartments, and then one day, these would-be-millionaires wake up on a park bench trying to remember how it came to be that someone else's curtains are hanging in their home and their door is sporting a new lock to which they don't have the key.

How the artist came to live in the cupboard under the stairs with no A/C (Amenities/Conveniences) is simple: the street cleaner rented him the overpriced room on credit, hoping that his tenant would someday win his lawsuit against Adik, the swindler who had commandeered his former apartment. But the lawsuit dragged on, and the artist's debt grew and grew. When the street cleaner would come in the morning to fetch his broom or his shovel and see the artist asleep without anything better to do, he'd grow annoyed—as would any honest worker who wakes up early and sees before him a lounging freeloader. The street cleaner would start shouting and the artist would pull the overcoat he'd been using as both mattress and blanket over his ears. Every day at seven o'clock sharp, the street cleaner would lament that he was the only idiot in the world who gave out apartments willy-nilly and then tolerated not being paid rent for six whole months!

"You owe me a million by now! I oughta kill you," screamed the street cleaner, brandishing his shovel above the artist's head. "Now pay up or get lost! I've got a whole waitlist of eager tenants! Or better yet," fantasized the street cleaner, "I could sell you! I'll post an ad: 'Slave for rent. Payment: three years up front.' But ads take time and money! That's it—go to the hospital and sell a kidney—you have two, what do you need them both for?" Their morning chats always ended the same way: "Get out," he'd say, "You've slept your money's worth! Go to the hospital!" Still half-asleep, the artist would drag himself outside wondering why his landlord was always sending him to the hospital. The street cleaner squawked every morning, just like a rooster. But unlike a rooster, he had weekends off, and that's when our poor artist could finally get some sleep.

After being thusly roused each morning, the artist would crawl out of his hole and roam the streets with the secret hope of finding a piece of bread or a hot cup of tea. Or he'd hang around the dumpster by his former apartment, hoping that Adik had thrown out all of his old things—his brushes, paints, and canvases—so he could finally paint something and sell it.

But when things are bad, they only get worse, and

one day, as the artist arrived at his former home, he saw a totally new family moving into his apartment, complete with a grand piano and a daughter holding a pack of five dogs on a leash while directing her father, mother, and four movers. They brought in books, shelves, sheet music, the grand piano, and then a cage holding a puffed-up cat that spurred the dogs to bark wildly (one of the dogs was obviously blind, but it barked along excitedly nonetheless). The artist immediately fell in love with the strange family, especially the blind dog and the girl in charge, so mature for her young age. He hung his head and walked off—he could never appear in court and demand the eviction of this family. Adik knew what he was doing when he sold them the apartment.

The artist set about his daily routine: he wandered the streets and painted. Yes, he still painted—though only in his mind. That's to say, he'd find a good vantage point and, like a general, observe his surroundings. On that day, for instance, a small house and a church, a cloud and a tree, a fat woman leaving the bakery with a baguette.

"Stay a while, you are so beautiful!" he'd quote to himself. In this painting, visible only to him, the colors were radiant and the world shone: the sky gleamed turquoise, the baguette and the walls of the church reflected gold, and the woman's dress bloomed magnificently, like a bouquet of lilacs. The crowning detail was a granny standing by the bakery door, wearing an orange flannel robe. Upon completing this masterpiece, the artist exhaled, his hands trembled, and his eyes glistened with tears of joy, because if the world could see his creation, it would undoubtedly laugh with delight. People would crowd around it in museums. He was sure of it!

Next, our dreamer would go to the bakery and inhale the aroma of fresh bread: the sweet, satisfying scent of rustic loaves and the toasty, airy smell of hot buns. It never crossed the artist's mind to beg for food or search for scraps on the floor; no, he just stood there with his eyes closed, warming his soul. Then he'd check his hiding place under the porch of a neighboring building, where he kept fragments of limestone, brick, and black charcoal. After that he'd search for an empty bit of sidewalk—he usually found some in the remotest corner of the park, where there weren't any guards or groundskeepers. The artist would crawl around on his knees until dark, drawing flowers, birds, cats, and dogs. He brought these creatures to life on the sidewalk—there was a sparrow perched by a cat and a brick-red poppy sprouting out of the pavement (as you may have guessed, the cat was white, the sparrow was gray, and their shadows were black as coal).

That day, after his hopes of winning back his apartment were dashed, the artist drew a pack of five dogs (one blind), a cage holding a white cat, and a grand piano. He drew the bossy daughter right under his feet, out of fear that otherwise she'd soon be trampled. Sometimes compassionate passersby would give him money, which is how he got by. This day, too, an audience gathered around his drawing—kids eating ice cream and their grandmothers equipped with the necessary provisions to contend with heat, rain, cold, or hunger; retirees wearing white and clutching newspapers to sit on in case of dirty benches; and empty-handed, unshaven men with signs of suffering on their faces. None of these people ever gave anything to our sidewalk artist. For that, there were middle-aged women who would burst into tears at the sight of a lonely, frail man. But the public didn't always approve of the sidewalk art. Many didn't like that the artist used only three colors. And some didn't like the way he drew.

"A photographer would do a better job," they'd say.

"I could've drawn that," they'd comment.

It was the children who were his most impressionable, enthusiastic audience, and they'd immediately rush to participate. Unfortunately, they weren't interested in doodling on the blank pavement (which was abundant) but instead wanted to scribble right on the artist's work. That day, some of the youngest covered his drawing with sand and dirt, then painstakingly brought over buckets of water from a nearby puddle and watered it while the rest happily sloshed about in the resulting swamp. The artist didn't object; he understood they were creating their own art out of dirt, which they trampled over with tiny feet. It was the grandmothers who objected—they leapt up from their benches and dragged away their grandchildren, bemoaning the wet feet, potential colds, and dirtied tights. So the children disappeared, leaving our artist alone with his muddy sidewalk. He thought this dirt art of tiny footprints was every bit as worthy of being in a museum as his own, though he wasn't quite sure which kind: a museum of contemporary art or of geology.

The children had drawn glasses and horns on the dogs, they'd watered the poppy so generously that it washed away, they'd played the grand piano with their feet, completely smudging it, and they'd even managed to mar the image of the young girl. And on top of that, no one had given him any money.

But then fate smiled down on the artist—he was approached by a man in a leather jacket with hands so dirty that his white nails stood out. The man was chewing gum and spat it out with remarkable precision: the wad landed right on the face of the bespectacled, horned, mustachioed girl at the artist's feet.

"Got a place for the night?" asked the man. "I'll pay. A lot."

"Money up front," said the starving artist. He figured that since it was Saturday, the street cleaner wouldn't be coming the next morning and he could share his room for one night. The man handed him a wad of small bills and demanded to be taken to his lodging. When they came to the cupboard under the stairs, the man took the key, disappeared behind the door, fell to the floor, and grew silent. After a moment, the artist heard a pathetic whistle, an asthmatic wheeze, and then a melancholy moan. He worried his tenant was suffocating in the windowless cupboard and tried opening the door but couldn't manage—the man was lying right up against it. The artist was about to break down the door when he heard the whistle, wheeze, and moan again. Then again and again—it was clear the man was asleep.

The artist politely retreated and took his wad of bills straight to the bakery, where he bought a pound of cheap bread, a fluffy bun, and even had enough for a bottle of crappy soda. With his belly full to the brim, he spent the day wandering the city, enjoying life, and in the evening returned to his cupboard. But he could not get in. Behind his door he heard a loud argument in an unfamiliar language, and his knocks weren't even noticed. Later that night, the door did open, but only to let in a woman carrying two enormous striped sacks. The artist tried to slip in after her but was pushed out by a number of hands and feet. He got the impression that there were at least five people in his cupboard, lying on top of bundles and bags

stacked up to the ceiling. The dejected artist lay down outside his door, shivering and miserable, and spent the whole
night listening to people snoring and arguing. There was
even an infant wailing—where he'd come from was a mys-
tery, maybe he'd just been born.

The next morning, three more women and their bags
moved into the cupboard. They disappeared behind the
door after stepping over the reposing artist, and soon the
stairwell filled with the smells of bread and salami. The
artist knocked on the door to discuss further payment and
was answered by a large fist adorned with a gold ring. The
fist waved around blindly, and the poor artist realized the
hopelessness of his situation—especially when more people began piling in, and then cramming the space in front
of his door with their things and their din while their children went through his pockets and someone began taking
off his overcoat. The frightened artist pulled himself free
and ran off.

There was nothing else to do but go about his usual
routine: paint in his mind, eat bread in his mind, etc.—the
happy life of a beggar. But our beggar was cold, sleep-de-
prived, and beginning to despair. He was furious with himself for being so gullible that he'd lost everything twice.

The artist didn't feel like painting with his eyes anymore, even though it was his favorite type of weather.
It was drizzling. A lilac-colored fog hung over the city,

breaking the colors around him into rainbows and obscur-
ing the objects in the distance, making them look mysterious. He used to love painting such scenes, especially in
watercolor. He'd wet a piece of paper in the nearest puddle, fix it to a board with some pushpins, and brush on a
golden sky (a mix of carbon black and cadmium orange),
then a gray horizon lined with colorful, blocky buildings.
His final flourish would be a car in the foreground, painted
bright emerald, its synthetic hue partially reflected in a
rippled puddle.

But now our hungry, wet, homeless artist ambled
about the city oblivious to the fog and the iridescent buildings. Everything that had once brought him joy was gone.
He was done dreaming about winning the lawsuit against
Adik or his paintings being hung in museums. He was
done pretending that everything was ahead of him and
that his only concern in the world was art. He was angry,
cold, and miserable.

The artist wandered the streets, resting on random
stoops and retreating into stores for warmth, when suddenly, right when he'd come to the end of his rope and was
ready to lie down and die, he felt compelled to return to
his old apartment. He fell asleep on his former doorstep,
waking in the morning only when he heard dogs barking
and smelled freshly brewed coffee wafting into the stairwell. Then came the beautiful sound of someone playing

the piano. Peeling his eyes open, the artist saw that next to him was a large jar of hot coffee and a paper bag. The bag contained a mound of fried potatoes, a bratwurst, a huge slice of bread, and a plastic fork. Oh, how joyfully our pauper savored this unexpected gift! How he wept, sitting outside his own door, grieving his cursed life! How he swore to turn things around so that one day he could thank the family by gifting them his sidewalk art: the bespectacled, horned, mustachioed girl surrounded by her horned, bespectacled dogs, all partially covered by sand and tiny footprints—his collaboration with the children in the park (most were good at drawing only mustaches and horns, while one very talented five-year-old had doodled all the glasses).

Just as the artist finished his breakfast, he heard the lock turning. He quickly grabbed the empty jar and bag and sped down the stairs. He couldn't face those kind people; he was ashamed he had needed their charity.

That evening, after many hours of roaming, the shivering artist took refuge beneath a random awning. It continued to rain, and he had nowhere to go. He would never go back to his former door, where he'd heard barking dogs and a piano. There was no point in returning to his cupboard, either. He sat there, eyes closed, waiting to be chased away (every awning belongs to someone). As expected, someone soon nudged him. The artist opened his eyes and saw an unfamiliar, portly man beaming at him. The man cheerfully declared that he was an old friend from art school—he even knew the artist's name and went on to explain that he no longer painted since becoming rich.

"Igor!" barked the so-called old friend. "Do you want my painting supplies? I've forgotten how to paint and I have no wish to remember. It makes such a mess, and I don't feel like getting dirty. But I see that you are in need."

"Supplies?" asked the artist. "Paint and paintbrushes?"

"Yes, Igor. And everything else."

"Canvases?"

"And more. Come with me."

It felt nice to be asked by someone to go somewhere—maybe it would be dry and warm there, maybe this mysterious Old Friend would give him something to eat and even a roof for the night. I've got nothing worth stealing, thought the artist. He sat before the stranger in thought, until the stranger said, "So, let's go?" But the artist felt uneasy about agreeing to such a random offer.

"Uh, I don't know . . . I'm in kind of a rush," he said.

"In a rush?" said the stranger, squirming irritably. "Where to?" he was yelling now, his foggy breath spilling from his mouth.

"I'm in a rush . . . sorry."

"You have nowhere to go!" The Old Friend smiled. "Don't you remember me? It's me, Izvosya! Remember? From school—I used to take your money!"

The artist instantly recognized him—the horrible bully Izvosya, who was two years his senior and did steal his money, pencils, and erasers.

"You have nowhere to go!" Izvosya kept yelling. "You're homeless! I went to your old apartment—I know everything. I've been looking for you! Adik got you, huh?" He began laughing, his breath still foggy. "There's even someone living in your cupboard!"

"I'm in a rush . . ."

Izvosya's face appeared to dissolve behind the mist of his breath. I think I'm losing my mind from hunger, thought the artist.

"Fine," came Izvosya's distant voice, "stay here. We're all our own worst enemy." And he melted into the evening haze. Yes, I've definitely lost my mind, thought the artist. He stood up from the stoop, for the first time noticing the building it was attached to: its windows and doors were missing, and in the entryway a small tree grew out of the crumbled floor. The artist walked inside, found an old couch in a corner, and, for the first time in days, fell asleep on something soft.

The next morning, he was yanked from his slumber

by a thundering sound—some sort of growling machine was knocking down the building's walls. No sooner had our artist darted outside than the roof collapsed. The artist shivered and went on his way, but he hadn't gone far before someone ran up behind him.

"Is this yours?" asked a stranger, panting. He handed him a canvas stretched over a frame. "I found it in your room."

The artist didn't have it in him to take something that wasn't his.

"No. That wasn't my room. It's not my canvas," he said shrugging. He continued on his way but then turned around after a few steps. The canvas lay abandoned by a concrete fence, and next to it was a small plywood case: unmistakably a folding easel. The fence was leaning precariously over these treasures—it, too, would collapse any minute. The artist couldn't resist; he ran back, grabbed the easel and canvas, and jumped away from the fence, which tumbled to the ground the next second.

He thought of Izvosya—he was a thief and a jerk who'd forced the artist to go hungry most schooldays, which is why the artist would never take anything from him. And he never took things that weren't his; he might've been a beggar, but he was no thief. This was a special case, though—you could say he had no choice but to save these precious items from destruction. He decided to take them to the city lost and found. He put the canvas under his arm and was lugging the heavy case (full of paints and brushes, by the feel of it) when he ran into a boisterous old woman with a plump, lively face.

"Do you know who lived in that apartment?" he asked her.

"An artist. He had just completed a commissioned portrait of an old friend when he suddenly died. He had no family. You should've seen what happened next—cars came from all over, there were guards stationed around the place! Us poor folk didn't get a thing: every last piece was snatched up by the rich!"

"Take this," said the artist, offering her his treasures.

"No, no. I already took a bunch of junk: paints, brushes, two rolls of canvas. No one at the market wanted it! I threw it all out. No one wants that stuff, not even artists—they use spray paint nowadays, don't they? Or give themselves paint enemas and then expel the goods straight onto a canvas! Brushes are ancient history, they told me." The surprisingly well-informed woman bounced cheerfully as she spoke, then quickly disappeared behind a corner.

Right away, the artist raced to his favorite spot, the bakery on the corner. He was met with a familiar sight: golden baguettes floated out of the bakery in people's arms and bags, a turquoise sky gleamed in the distance (it had finally stopped raining and the air was warm), there was a small church with a silver dome, and beyond it towered pink, green, and yellow apartment buildings. The same granny in the orange robe hobbled toward the bakery.

The artist set up his easel and got to work. The brushes flashed in his hands and the canvas soon shone with light and color. Passersby stopped and said things like, "The bread isn't right," or "The sky is all wrong,"— which is to say, things were back to normal. He'd heard such comments many times before and no longer paid them any mind. Adik, too, had once come up to the artist on the street. But he had acted differently from the others, excessively praising a barely started painting. (And we all know how good it feels when an impartial viewer, someone who's an expert and a real connoisseur, appreciates our work.) Naturally, the artist had invited Adik to his home to look at his other paintings. Adik was impressed once again. He wanted to help the talented artist sell his apartment for a profit and buy himself a cheaper one—it was obvious the artist was in debt (paint isn't cheap, and no one buys paintings). Of course, the artist wasn't capable of orchestrating such a complicated transaction on his own, so he gave Adik power of attorney over all of his property that very day. We already know how that ended: the artist was soon sleeping on a park bench.

Having quickly finished his painting, the artist decided to go see his lawyer about the lawsuit against Adik. He rushed off and then turned around to say a quick goodbye to his beloved place. But he could no longer see anything—not the church, not the bakery, not even the colorful apartment buildings. A leaden fog had descended, blanketing everything that he had just painted. Funny how fast the weather changes, thought the artist absentmindedly, and continued on his way. Surprisingly, his lawyer was available.

"It looks like your case has been won," he said. "Adik will be evicted from your apartment today. Don't forget, you owe me 10 percent, and don't wait too long—your debt will grow every day." The artist was so ecstatic he didn't realize what his victory meant until he was outside. He stopped cold in his tracks. It wasn't Adik who would be evicted today, but the family—the girl and her parents, five dogs, and cat! The artist rushed back to the lawyer's office, but he had already left for the day. The artist wanted to sign away his apartment to the current tenants, but he couldn't get the paperwork—that department's office wasn't taking appointments that day.

Things grew more dismal from there—when he arrived at his former home he was met with commotion. Dogs were barking, the door stood ajar, and it was clear the tenants were gathering their things. The artist walked into his apartment and saw the girl cramming the cat into the cage.

"Stop! You don't have to move out," he said to her. "You should stay!"

"What?" The girl frowned—the cat had splayed its hind legs and wouldn't fit through the cage's narrow door.

"I am the owner of this apartment. I just got it back. You're welcome to live here."

"I see," said the girl indifferently. "So, you're the person who robbed Adik? Took everything from him and put him in jail? Then felt bad and gave him one of your apartments? That's you?"

"What? Adik is the crook," said the baffled artist.

"Adik?" repeated the girl coldly, finally stuffing the cat into the cage. "Adik is my husband." She said this without any resentment or pride, but with a certain force. As if someone had doubted it was true. As she carried the cat out of the room, the artist noticed that she had a limp.

"Let me help you, your leg is hurt," he said.

"My leg isn't hurt."

"I can see that it is."

"I am not hurt," said the girl. She dragged the cage downstairs, clearly making an effort not to limp.

The movers were already slipping straps under the grand piano and the apartment was gradually emptying. The artist—what else was he to do—started helping. He picked up some chairs and even tied together a few books when the girl's father showed up and said something to the movers. They left immediately, as did the father (a confused-looking man with a beard), and all that remained was the grand piano, a table, and a bookshelf standing among bits of loose trash. Downstairs, a car roared and drove off. The artist looked out the window and saw the whole family out on the sidewalk sitting atop their suitcases; the girl had the cat cage on her lap and the dogs lay fanned out around them. It looked like they were waiting for someone.

It had been a miserable, rainy spring that year; at that particular time of day, the clouds hung low in a dense mass, like an overfilled hot-water bottle draped atop the city, and there was no doubt this rubber sky would soon burst. The artist was afraid to go downstairs, afraid to offer his help. The family was probably waiting for Adik, but Adik didn't come. The artist saw the girl get out two bowls, fill them with kibble, and extract the cat from its cage. The animals began eating lunch—the dogs obediently took turns as the cat ate off to the side, and still the family remained seated on their suitcases. It began to drizzle.

The artist felt so guilty, he didn't even dare show his face in the window. When misfortunes befell him, he tried not to think about them and went on with his life, cherishing the rare happy moments. That's to say he concentrated on the present—hiding from the rain, finding some loose change or a good scrap of bread in the trash—and didn't think too far ahead. If it had been his parents who were homeless and sitting on the street in the rain, he would have lost his mind! In this case, though, his hands were tied. Adik had robbed and abandoned his wife, sold her apartment with the promise of finding a better place, then relocated her to the artist's attic apartment—and now the poor girl didn't want to hear a word against her Adik. He'd probably harped on how he was in a tight spot, was being followed, his life threatened, and so on. The artist was reflecting on all this when Adik himself appeared behind him.

"I'm taking the keys," he said. "I've appealed to a higher court and, for now, this is still my apartment. I have it on record that you owe me a large sum of money and this apartment is your collateral. I still have that power of attorney, remember? Now get out of here, you bastard, or I'll have you killed! My guys only swing twice: once to whack you, once to nail your coffin shut. But not you—you won't get buried. They'll throw your body in the dump for the strays or in the pond for the fish. Got it?"

"Your wife told me you sold her apartment. Is that true?"

"What wife?" asked Adik.

"The girl with the dogs. With the hurt leg."

"Limping Vera?" Adik cackled. "She's got an imagination on her. She's not my wife. Ha! 'Wives' like her are a dime a dozen. Anyway, get lost. I've already resold this apartment to a family of New Russians."

Familiar voices sounded from the stairs. He heard cursing, yelling, and laughter. An infant was crying, his wails drawing nearer.

"Wait," said the artist. "Adik, did these new people pay you up front?"

"Why do you care?"

"Because their money is fake—you hear me? They'll arrest you before you get the bills out of your pocket," the artist lied enthusiastically. Adik glanced down at his bulging breast pocket; it was so stuffed that it hung over his shirt like an old balcony on a house.

"Adik, I rented them my room, they paid me, I went to the store to buy some bread, and the cashier raised hell. I ran."

"Right," said Adik quickly. "You stay here and don't let anyone in. I was never here, got it?"

"Give me the key, I'll lock up," demanded the artist, getting to the door just in time. There was a pounding at the door and screaming in the stairwell. Adik grew pale.

"What now?" he whispered, covered in sweat.

"Hey! Open up!" someone yelled.

"I'll guard the apartment," the artist said. "You get

Vera and her family off the street—or else they'll track you down through them."

"But how? How do I get out of here?"

"Use the fire escape to get to the roof."

Adik darted to the window, adding, "I installed steel window bars—lock them behind me or they'll climb in!"

The door shook from the pounding, but it, too, was steel and double reinforced—another of Adik's additions. The artist barred all the windows, and now that he couldn't look down at the street, he decided to work. He went to his easel and began painting right over his previous work—after all, he didn't have another canvas. A short while later—after he'd laid out the first sketches of the girl, her parents, the cat, and the dogs—he opened a window, threw open the bars, and looked down. The street was empty except for a man with an umbrella.

The artist went back to living in his apartment. He painted, sustaining himself on leftover grains he'd found in the kitchen, and listened to the lively happenings outside his door. The cupboard family had made themselves at home on the stairs—there was singing and guitar playing, there were small children running around like ponies and loud arguments provoked by tenants from the lower floors. It seemed like someone had even taken up residence in the elevator and, judging by the commotion, it was the patriarch of this huge family; the stairway dwellers were constantly yelling, "In the elevator! Roman is in the elevator! Go ask Roman! He's in there sleeping!" The artist imagined the scene vividly: the new tenants lying and sitting on the stairs, each step descending like the seats in a theater, and in the elevator—as if in the center of a stage—Roman perched atop a pillow in his leather jacket, the gold ring glinting on his finger.

But none of this concerned our artist; he was busy painting. He felt like the former tenants, his beloved family, now belonged to him. He could even change the girl's expression at will—one day she'd look at him mockingly, her eyes narrowed, and the next day her face would be cheerful and loving. He made small improvements, like giving the blind dog one eye and painting a roomier cage for the cat.

One morning, when the artist had just cooked up his last handful of semolina and opened the last can of cat food that smelled vaguely of meat, Adik appeared in his barred window. He patiently stood outside on the fire escape and tapped at the glass like a docile pigeon. The artist walked up to the window, chewing the cat food, and shook his head.

"Let me in!" Adik yelled.

"No way," said the artist.

"Fine, what do you want?"

"Marry Vera! You hear me?"

"You're crazy!" yelled Adik.

"Listen up! There's three years' worth of food here, there's gas, there's water, and the apartment is mine," said the artist, his voice booming.

"And if I marry her, you'll give me the apartment?"

"Yes!"

"Well, damn, then I'll marry her tomorrow. Where is she?"

"But the apartment will be only in her name, without the right to resell. Got it?"

Without another word, Adik leapt off the windowsill and disappeared over the roofs. From their conversation, the artist realized with horror that Vera and her parents weren't living with Adik. Where had they disappeared to?

He had to find them. Forgetting everything, he opened the door to walk out of his apartment. He had planned to lock up, but in an instant, the stairwell dwellers flooded into his apartment like water through a broken dam. They streamed into the hallway and spilled into the rooms: people with children, knapsacks, featherbeds, bags, pillows, and samovars. They cursed and argued about who'd get which room. A crash sounded from the back—someone must've opened the grand piano and jumped inside while several others, all at once, pounded on the keys. The last to enter was the massive Roman, carrying a pillow. He was dripping in gold jewelry, wearing jeans, sneakers, and the leather jacket, and his cheek, still red from sleeping, had a down feather stuck to it. He peeked into a few rooms then disappeared into the bathroom, surprisingly still unoccupied.

A moment ago, this was an empty, barren apartment, but now the floor was covered in people sleeping, old men's noses sticking up from pillows, and children running right atop the reclining bodies. From the kitchen came domestic squabbling—the kind that happens when multiple matriarchs are cooking at once—and the sound of water pouring and the clanking of pots and dishes.

"You hungry?" a portly granny wrapped in multiple shawls asked the artist.

"No, thank you," he said and returned to his art room. There were children crowded around his painting. Someone had opened the paint tubes, and the result was horrifying: the children looked like housepainters, with paint-splattered hair, faces, arms, legs, and pants. When they saw the artist, the children leapt away from the painting, revealing that it was now covered in a thick layer of red paint, like blood. The precious family portrait was irreparably ruined.

The artist sighed and reflexively began painting over it. Eyes began to appear on the crimson canvas—lively, curious, gleaming children's eyes; crinkled elderly eyes; huge girls' eyes; and cunning women's eyes. Then the artist added the knapsacks, mattresses, skirts, shawls, and windowsills piled high with pots and jars. He painted the copper samovar, already boiling, standing on a white table-cloth laden with red teacups; piles of golden, ring-shaped rolls; a dish of raspberry jam; a jar of pickles; a mound of sliced rye bread; and a gold-trimmed ruby teapot the size of a milk jug.

"Paint me! Paint me!" yelped the children, and the artist generously painted each one as the whole flock of tenants crowded around him. The artist was so engrossed in his work, he didn't notice the time pass. When the painting was almost finished, he heard a distant, fright-ened cry behind him. He turned around and saw that the room had emptied except for one small girl who sat weep-ing in its farthest corner. She held a newborn in her arms. The artist understood that the girl felt left out and quickly found a spot for her on his canvas: he painted her—her skirt, her beaded necklace, her tears, her curls, and her bony arms clutching the tiny, sleeping infant. Then he painted the infant's pink cheeks, thick eyelashes, and the dark fuzz on his doll-sized head.

Once the artist had transferred them onto his canvas, a heavy silence settled over the apartment. The artist wiped off his brushes and looked around. Emptiness. The girl and the infant were gone. A lone cloth bundle lay in the corner, the ornate lid of a samovar peeking out. The artist forced himself to add this samovar to the bottom of his painting. Now he could take a breath. As he walked around his apartment, he discovered that the samovar was gone, too. The family must've run off, taking everything with them. Maybe they were frightened of being painted? The artist checked whether his guests had closed the door behind them, then, for extra security, he locked the deadbolt.

His apartment was completely empty, save for some trash littering the floor. Then he heard a familiar snore—whistling, wheezing, and moaning—coming from the bathroom. He opened the door and saw the massive Roman asleep in the tub on a pile of featherbeds, fully clothed and belly up.

"How'd I miss the elephant in the room?" cried the artist, rushing to add Roman to his masterpiece. He found room for him atop a pile of mattresses above the grand piano. It was a surprisingly easy task: just a dozen strokes and the sleeping head of this family appeared in all his glory, levitating above his people. Having painted Roman, the artist peeked into the bathroom to see if it had worked. The towering bed was empty. Then, the artist checked the deadbolt, which convinced him that no one had left the apartment.

The artist sat on the floor, genuinely frightened. Had

the family disappeared into his painting? And what about the others: the woman with the baguette? The hobbling granny in the orange robe by the bakery door? The family with the cat and five dogs? Had they all gone to the same place?

The artist had long felt that the subjects of his paintings sort of dissolved, deteriorated, faded, after his work was complete. Roses wilted, people grew pale, the sky turned colorless—it was no longer the same glowing sky he'd captured on his canvas. And the artist had been secretly proud that only his paintings were able to preserve that magical light.

He had painted the family with the dogs so that they could live forever—same with the bakery on the corner and his itinerant tenants. He used to think. Tomorrow will be a new day, with a new sun and new vistas. God has plenty of everything. But now, after the disappearance of Roman and the samovar, the artist was plagued by terrible thoughts and suspicions. The canvas and paint—could these gifts have come from his terrifying Old Friend? Even the most harmless object can become lethal if wielded by malicious hands, let alone something as complex as art, through which an artist can stop time and immortalize any subject while he himself might die like a stray in the streets—ridiculed, penniless, and insane! (Ask any historian; they know of many such cases.)

The artist stared at his painting in horror. Staring back at him was the cupboard family, whom he might have just murdered. Their sad, dark eyes seemed to be pleading for something. Stricken, the artist gathered the easel and paints, grabbed his painting, and ran out the door. He raced to his favorite corner, to the bakery.

It was nowhere to be found.

In its place was some sort of large-scale construction site. The sidewalk had been replaced by a gaping abyss, and towering all around it were construction vehicles and piles of earth. The artist stood before the freshly dug grave that had swallowed up his favorite spot and shuddered. He finally understood his Old Friend's gift. Whatever was painted on the canvas would never return.

The world was coming to an end. How many more of these canvases had the Old Friend scattered in art stores? How many artists would be duped into buying these cheap instruments of death? He understood that he couldn't throw away the canvas or the paint, lest someone else claim them. So the artist dragged his deadly burden down the city streets, hoping to find the place where these dangerous gifts had been foisted upon him.

As he walked, his path was blocked again and again by fresh rubble and colossal, thrashing beasts of machinery. He was desperate to find Izvosya make a deal: if Izvosya would take back his paraphernalia and restore everyone the artist had painted, the artist would offer the greedy bully his apartment (he'd never be able to pay his lawyer anyway). Or Izvosya could take his life—what was the point of living if Vera and her family were gone?

At last, the artist reached the godforsaken place (he was sure of it—he had a photographic memory). This was where the street had ended at a crumbling fence and a decrepit building, but now there stood a looming mansion with a five-story tower, balconies, and a red-tiled roof. It was surrounded by a solid concrete wall topped with barbed wire. The artist rang the doorbell by the metal door set in the wall but was answered only by barking dogs. Every time he rang the bell, the dogs would wail as if they were being electrocuted, but otherwise the mansion remained silent and unmoving.

Purely out of habit, the artist took the easel off his shoulder and set it up; he squeezed some paint onto his palette, poured some paint-thinner in a cup, propped up the cursed canvas, and began painting over his last work. He roughly outlined the mansion and concrete wall; he added cold, blue shadows and warm-hued dabs of light and sketched some sparse greenery around the house and colorful curtains in the windows. He didn't leave a single thing out (bar the raven sitting on the edge of the roof—he didn't want to murder an innocent bird).

Suddenly, the curtains in one of the windows parted,

and he saw the flash of a pale face with an open mouth. The artist quickly dashed off a whitish speck with a black dot and the face disappeared. A small, black shape glinted in another window—the artist's brush rendered that, too, and the black glint disappeared. It had been a gun.

Now he needed to carefully paint the details. He began with the lowest row of windows. And as he painted, the mansion began to dissolve. The tower grew transparent, the roof's white rafters were left exposed, and the frightened raven took flight and began circling the mansion, which was melting like a sugar cube in a cup of tea.

After completing the wall, which immediately disappeared, the artist saw a robe coming toward him holding a bundle of leashes, ready to release a pack of furious, snarling dogs. It took only two seconds to paint the dogs, who without taking a single step ended up on the canvas in their menacing poses. Of course, the artist didn't paint the sky, the forest on the horizon, or the neighboring houses—and certainly not the small herd of goats and the old woman sitting on a stump.

"You!" said the headless body in the velvet robe and gold slippers. The voice came from above the shoulders, where, instead of a head, the artist could see the top of a distant lilac bush in bloom. "Igor, pal, let's talk!"

"Wait," said the artist, and finished painting the headless body. Now all he could see was the lilac bush in its full height, unobstructed. His painting depicted the mansion, a tiny yelling head in one of its windows, and the head's body towering in the foreground in an impressive robe and gold slippers.

"And what's the point of all this?" yelped Izvosya's voice out of nowhere. "I can't help you without a body. I can only destroy you. I can't bring your friends back to life in this state. Erase me from the painting and I'll do anything."

"Okay then, destroy me."

"Are you crazy? I'm your old friend!"

"Fine. If you free everyone else I painted, I'll free you. I want them back right this minute."

"Now we're talking. I knew you were an honest guy; you always handed over your money without a fight. Now I'll repay you. Say the magic words: 'Ciao ciao bambino!' The last to disappear will be the first to come back. The rest, you'll find where you left them, I swear!"

"Ciao ciao bambino!" said the artist. Instantly, the canvas went blank. The mansion reappeared in its place, and then came the joyful mob, led by Roman. They overtook the concrete wall in a flash and paraded into the mansion along with their samovars, featherbeds, and children. Their faces flashed in the windows and on the balconies. The mansion's owner, having appeared out of thin air, rushed to release his resurrected dogs, but, luckily, the artist was quick to paint Izvosya and his dogs back on the canvas from memory (he had a photographic memory, after all). The mansion's balconies were already strung with wet laundry, smoke billowed from the chimney, and children shouted in the yard—everything was as it should be.

"Come on, say 'Ciao ciao bambino' again!" said a sad voice. "Say it! Or else I'll be whispering in your ear forever."

"Go ahead, I'll plug it up," said the artist. He threw his painting supplies over the fence and heard the gleeful yelps of children as they pounced on the plywood case and ripped the canvas to shreds.

The artist ran home and found his beloved family sitting on their suitcases just as before—the animals were still eating lunch, and the family was still awaiting someone. The artist hid just inside his building and watched as the girl used a pay phone, had a quick conversation, then returned to her parents with a shocked expression.

"Adik said that if I give him the apartment of some man named Igor, he will marry me after all. He didn't even say hello, just declared: 'Will marry for apartment. Stamped and signed, your Adik, your dream.'" Her parents laughed quietly. After thinking it over, the girl laughed, too. The artist walked out onto the sidewalk.

"Your apartment is free," he said. "Here are the keys." He picked up a stack of books in each hand. And just like that, the family grabbed all their suitcases, Vera collected the bowls off the ground and pulled the dogs' leashes, and everyone went to the elevator.

After that, it's fair to say the artist's life took a turn for the better. He eventually married his lovely Vera, but not before warning her that he paints only abstracts—never people or landscapes—and that it never earns him much. Lastly, he mentioned that from time to time he hears a reproachful voice whispering from nowhere, and has to plug his ears.

"Just a little quirk."

To which Vera replied, "You've always been and always will be my quirky man!"

Thank you all
for your support.
We do this for you,
and could not do
it without you.

DEEP
VELLUM

PARTNERS

pixel ▐▐▐ texel

ADDITIONAL DONORS, CONT'D

Mark Haber
Mary Cline
Maynard Thomson
Michael Reklis
Mike Soto
Mokhtar Ramadan
Nikki & Dennis Gibson
Patrick Kukucka
Patrick Kutcher
Rev. Elizabeth & Neil Moseley
Richard Meyer

Scott & Katy Nimmons
Sherry Perry
Sydneyann Binion
Stephen Harding
Stephen Williamson
Susan Carp
Susan Ernst
Theater Jones
Tim Perttula
Tony Thomson

SUBSCRIBERS

Ned Russin
Michael Binkley
Michael Schneiderman
Aviya Kushner
Kenneth McClain
Eugenie Cha
Stephen Fuller
Joseph Rebella
Brian Matthew Kim

Anthony Brown
Michael Lighty
Erin Kubatzky
Shelby Vincent
Margaret Terwey
Ben Fountain
Caroline West
Ryan Todd
Gina Rios

Caitlin Jans
Ian Robinson
Elena Rush
Courtney Sheedy
Elif Ağanoğlu
Laura Gee
Valerie Boyd
Brian Bell

AVAILABLE NOW FROM DEEP VELLUM

MICHÈLE AUDIN · *One Hundred Twenty-One Days* · translated by Christiana Hills · FRANCE

BAE SUAH · *Recitation* · translated by Deborah Smith · SOUTH KOREA

MARIO BELLATIN · *Mrs. Murakami's Garden* · translated by Heather Cleary · MEXICO

EDUARDO BERTI · *The Imagined Land* · translated by Charlotte Coombe · ARGENTINA

CARMEN BOULLOSA · *Texas: The Great Theft* · *Before* · *Heavens on Earth*
translated by Samantha Schnee · Peter Bush · Shelby Vincent · MEXICO

MAGDA CARNECI · *FEM* · translated by Sean Cotter · ROMANIA

LEILA S. CHUDORI · *Home* · translated by John H. McGlynn · INDONESIA

MATHILDE CLARK · *Lone Star* · translated by Martin Aitken · DENMARK

SARAH CLEAVE, ed. · *Banthology: Stories from Banned Nations* ·
IRAN, IRAQ, LIBYA, SOMALIA, SUDAN, SYRIA & YEMEN

LOGEN CURE · *Welcome to Midland: Poems* · USA

ANANDA DEVI · *Eve Out of Her Ruins* · translated by Jeffrey Zuckerman · MAURITIUS

PETER DIMOCK · *Daybook from Sheep Meadow* · USA

CLAUDIA ULLOA DONOSO · *Little Bird,* translated by Lily Meyer · PERU/NORWAY

ROSS FARRAR · *Ross Sings Cheree & the Animated Dark: Poems* · USA

ALISA GANIEVA · *Bride and Groom* · *The Mountain and the Wall*
translated by Carol Apollonio · RUSSIA

FERNANDA GARCIA LAU · *Out of the Cage* · translated by Will Vanderhyden · ARGENTINA

ANNE GARRÉTA · *Sphinx* · *Not One Day* · *In/concrete* · translated by Emma Ramadan · FRANCE

JÓN GNARR · *The Indian* · *The Pirate* · *The Outlaw* · translated by Lytton Smith · ICELAND

GOETHE · *The Golden Goblet: Selected Poems* · *Faust, Part One*
translated by Zsuzsanna Ozsváth and Frederick Turner · GERMANY

NOEMI JAFFE · *What are the Blind Men Dreaming?* · translated by Julia Sanches & Ellen Elias-Bursac · BRAZIL

CLAUDIA SALAZAR JIMÉNEZ · *Blood of the Dawn* · translated by Elizabeth Bryer · PERU

PERGENTINO JOSÉ · *Red Ants* · MEXICO

TAISIA KITAISKAIA · *The Nightgown & Other Poems* · USA

JUNG YOUNG MOON · *Seven Samurai Swept Away in a River* · *Vaseline Buddha*
translated by Yewon Jung · SOUTH KOREA

KIM YIDEUM · *Blood Sisters* · translated by Ji yoon Lee · SOUTH KOREA

JOSEFINE KLOUGART · *Of Darkness* · translated by Martin Aitken · DENMARK

YANICK LAHENS · *Moonbath* · translated by Emily Gogolak · HAITI

FOUAD LAROUI · *The Curious Case of Dassoukine's Trousers* · translated by Emma Ramadan · MOROCCO

MARIA GABRIELA LLANSOL · *The Geography of Rebels Trilogy: The Book of Communities; The Remaining Life; In the House of July & August* translated by Audrey Young · PORTUGAL

PABLO MARTÍN SÁNCHEZ · *The Anarchist Who Shared My Name* · translated by Jeff Diteman · SPAIN

DOROTA MASŁOWSKA · *Honey, I Killed the Cats* · translated by Benjamin Paloff · POLAND

BRICE MATTHIEUSSENT· *Revenge of the Translator* · translated by Emma Ramadan · FRANCE

LINA MERUANE · *Seeing Red* · translated by Megan McDowell · CHILE

VALÉRIE MRÉJEN · *Black Forest* · translated by Katie Shireen Assef · FRANCE

FISTON MWANZA MUJILA · *Tram 83* · translated by Roland Glasser · DEMOCRATIC REPUBLIC OF CONGO

GORAN PETROVIĊ · *At the Lucky Hand, aka The Sixty-Nine Drawers* · translated by Peter Agnone · SERBIA

ILJA LEONARD PFEIJFFER · *La Superba* · translated by Michele Hutchison · NETHERLANDS

RICARDO PIGLIA · *Target in the Night* · translated by Sergio Waisman · ARGENTINA

SERGIO PITOL · *The Art of Flight · The Journey · The Magician of Vienna · Mephisto's Waltz: Selected Short Stories* translated by George Henson · MEXICO

JULIE POOLE · *Bright Specimen: Poems from the Texas Herbarium* · USA

EDUARDO RABASA · *A Zero-Sum Game* · translated by Christina MacSweeney · MEXICO

ZAHIA RAHMANI · *"Muslim": A Novel* · translated by Matthew Reeck · FRANCE/ALGERIA

JUAN RULFO · *The Golden Cockerel & Other Writings* · translated by Douglas J. Weatherford · MEXICO

ETHAN RUTHERFORD · *Farthest South & Other Stories* · USA

TATIANA RYCKMAN · *Ancestry of Objects* · USA

OLEG SENTSOV · *Life Went On Anyway* · translated by Uilleam Blacker · UKRAINE

MIKHAIL SHISHKIN · *Calligraphy Lesson: The Collected Stories* translated by Marian Schwartz, Leo Shtutin, Mariya Bashkatova, Sylvia Maizell · RUSSIA

ÓFEIGUR SIGURÐSSON · *Öræfi: The Wasteland* · translated by Lytton Smith · ICELAND

DANIEL SIMON, ED. · *Dispatches from the Republic of Letters* · USA

MUSTAFA STITOU · *Two Half Faces* · translated by David Colmer · NETHERLANDS

MÄRTA TIKKANEN · *The Love Story of the Century* · translated by Stina Katchadourian · SWEDEN

SERHIY ZHADAN · *Voroshilovgrad* · translated by Reilly Costigan-Humes & Isaac Wheeler · UKRAINE

FORTHCOMING FROM DEEP VELLUM

SHANE ANDERSON · *After the Oracle* · USA

MARIO BELLATIN · *Beauty Salon* · translated by David Shook · MEXICO

MIRCEA CĂRTĂRESCU · *Solenoid*
translated by Sean Cotter · ROMANIA

LEYLÂ ERBIL · *A Strange Woman*
translated by Nermin Menemencioğlu & Amy Marie Spangler· TURKEY

RADNA FABIAS · *Habitus* · translated by David Colmer · CURAÇAO/NETHERLANDS

SARA GOUDARZI · *The Almond in the Apricot* · USA

GYULA JENEI · *Always Different* · translated by Diana Senechal · HUNGARY

UZMA ASLAM KHAN • *The Miraculous True History of Nomi Ali* • PAKISTAN

SONG LIN · *The Gleaner Song: Selected Poems* · translated by Dong Li · CHINA

TEDI LÓPEZ MILLS · *The Book of Explanations* · translated by Robin Myers · MEXICO

JUNG YOUNG MOON · *Arriving in a Thick Fog*
translated by Mah Eunji and Jeffrey Karvonen · SOUTH KOREA

FISTON MWANZA MUJILA · *The Villain's Dance*, translated by Roland Glasser · *The River in the Belly: Selected Poems*, translated by Bret Maney · DEMOCRATIC REPUBLIC OF CONGO

LUDMILLA PETRUSHEVSKAYA · *Kidnapped: A Crime Story*, translated by Marian Schwartz · *The New Adventures of Helen: Magical Tales*, translated by Jane Bugaeva · RUSSIA

SERGIO PITOL · *The Love Parade* · translated by G. B. Henson · MEXICO

MANON STEFAN ROS · *The Blue Book of Nebo* · WALES

JIM SCHUTZE · *The Accommodation* · USA

SOPHIA TERAZAWA · *Winter Phoenix: Testimonies in Verse* · POLAND

BOB TRAMMELL · *Jack Ruby & the Origins of the Avant-Garde in Dallas & Other Stories* · USA

BENJAMIN VILLEGAS · *ELPASO: A Punk Story* · translated by Jay Noden · MEXICO